Angel of Justice

By

A J Weir

Published by Sammon Publishing Ltd

ISBN 0-9540031-5-2

First Edition 2003

PO BOX 3841

Bracknell

Berkshire

RG42 1PU

123456789

© AJ Weir 30.6.03

International Rights held by Sammon Publishing Ltd
Cover design and illustrations copyright Kathy Pinto
Music copyright Miles Willshire

Also from Sammon Publishing Ltd

JOHN WAYNE: A GIANT SHADOW   McGivern   ISBN 0 ~ 9540031 ~ 0 ~ 1

THE CAVALRY OFFICER   Thornton   ISBN 0 ~ 9540031 ~ 1 ~ X

OUT OF SCHOOL   edited by McGivern   ISBN 0 ~ 9540031 ~ 4 ~ 4

ALL SHARED
ALL BELONG
ALL IMPORTANT
ALL LIVE

IN THE NAME OF JUSTICE FOREVER

Angel of Justice - Fanfare

Miles Willshire

For Gordon, Jamie and Abbey...

because...

*With special thanks to Carolyn,
Kathy, AndrewM, Dominic,
Sarah, Diane, Jane,
Andrew W, Mrs Methven,
Miles, John,
Laura, Caroline
and the many other friends and
family who have helped.*

Contents

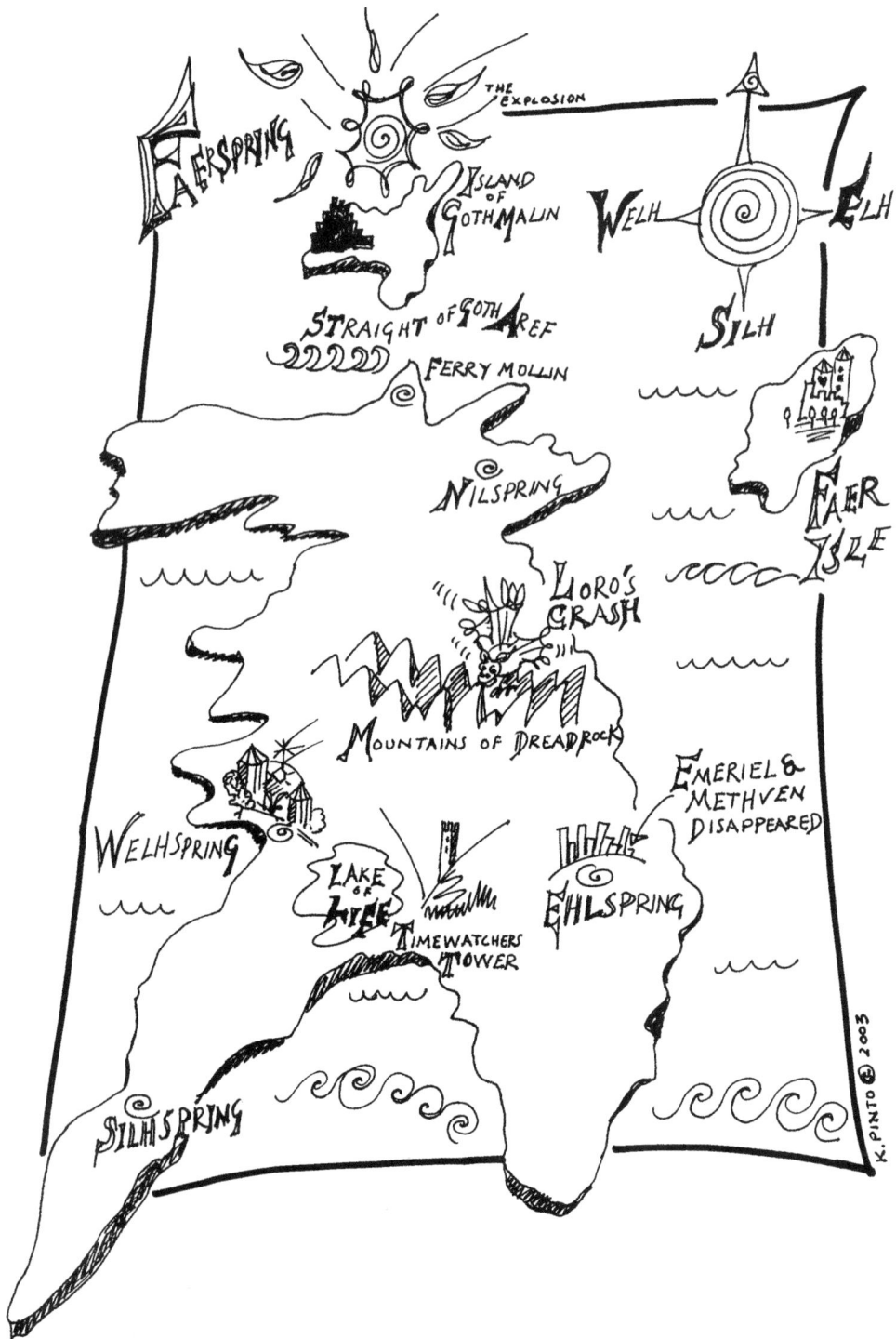

FAERSPRING

THE EXPLOSION

WELH   ELH

SILH

Island of GOTHMALIN

STRAIGHT OF GOTHAREF

FERRY MOLLIN

NILSPRING

FAER ISLE

LIORO'S CRASH

Mountains of DREADROCK

EMERIEL & METHVEN DISAPPEARED

WELHSPRING

LAKE OF LIFE

TIMEWATCHERS TOWER

EHLSPRING

SILHSPRING

K. PINTO © 2003

Chapter One

The Secret

"That's the second time he's disappeared like that!" Ellie commented to Jo. They were lying on the ground next to the ivy-clad bench at the bottom of their grandmother's wild, rambling, garden.

"What?" Jo murmured lazily, engrossed in constructing the final link in the daisy chain for the restless and unappreciative Scrap. He was Grandma's favourite, a Jack Russell Terrier who hated to be still, even for a second and was desperate to be gone.

"Jo! Ellie! Where are you? Look what I've found!" Tom called to them. He sounded distant, too distant, considering they had seen him only seconds ago in the nearby ferns. Ellie couldn't help wondering what trouble he'd unearthed this time. Scrap scampered off in the direction of Tom's voice, needing little excuse.

"We're coming, Tom!" Jo yelled. "We're coming!" She tripped clumsily as she raced off behind Scrap.

"Over here!" he exclaimed excitedly. They found him with Scrap, standing in a mossy, fern-covered dell, just high enough for a tall eleven-year-old boy and just wide enough for the three of them to stand side by side. Small shafts of sunlight pierced one corner of the dark green hidey-hole. Isolated from the usual sounds of the garden, it was eerily still, peaceful and as though this place held a mysterious secret. The three, usually very noisy, chattering children, fell silent, glancing around anxiously.

Then they heard the familiar but distant sound of the hand bell, which Grandma rang at her back door to summon them from whatever activity was occupying them. It broke the silence; relieved, they ran at top speed through the overgrown ferns and sapling silver birches to the rickety wooden fence.

Jo stopped abruptly, "Scrap… Where's Scrap?" Tom and Ellie halted, starting to call the absent dog. There was no response. Normally he would appear from some rabbit hole or other with a suitably muddy nose. Occasionally if he had found something more interesting he did not. Today he did not!

Ellie glared at Tom furiously, "This is all your fault. He followed you into that place. Why do you always get us into trouble? Grandma will be mad."

"Look! It's nothing to do with me if that stupid dog…" He retorted angrily as Jo interrupted.

"Shut up, you two! We've got to find Scrap." She was distressed at Scrap's loss and could not understand why they had to choose now to get into an argument.

Jo's love for animals often overtook her at such moments. She was usually placid and quiet with a carefree outlook.

Ellie and Tom paused briefly, knowing she was right. "You'll have to go back and get him, Tom. He was in the hidey-hole: he's probably still there!" Ellie said.

The bell rang again, more insistently.

Ellie and Jo hurried down the long grassy hill, past the purple heather and the ancient well, racing helter-skelter across the concrete by the empty stable block and along the path by grandma's flower beds to the back door.

Breathlessly, they tumbled into her cuddly figure, as she looked down at them and said, "Lunch time! Now come on in and tell me what you've been up to, dears."

"Nothing!" They replied simultaneously and quite unconvincingly.

"Where's Tom?" Grandma asked suspiciously, scanning the garden.

Tom was still at the entrance to the hidey-hole, looking for Scrap as instructed by his older sister. There was a shimmering glow around the entrance, but he could hear Scrap growling and, ignoring the odd sight, he dashed in. He stepped into a void of spiralling colours. No mossy floor, no fern ceiling, just a bottomless shadowy emptiness! He could just make out Scrap in the distant gloom, yelping and clearly terrified. Suddenly a large bat flew at Tom with alarming speed; strange looking with a deep red head and enormous fangs. Tom, now under attack, fought back bravely, foolishly some might say, but that was Tom, never considering the outcome. The bat viciously bit his arm. Tom pulled away as the horrifying bat lunged again. He landed in a heap at the entrance. His arm was agonisingly painful and blood dripped steadily from the open jagged wound.

The bell rang with agitation and Tom ran for his life, partly from fear of the red headed bat and partly from fear of his kindly, but firm Grandma. He sped down the hill. How was he going to hide the wound and how would he rescue Scrap? Glancing around, he spotted and snatched an old rag dangling from the rickety fence. He hastily bound his wound and fled down the hill, arriving breathlessly in front of his frowning Grandma.

"Sorry, Grandma. Scrap ran off."

Grandma had trained Scrap lovingly and diligently as a puppy, she knew this was unlikely. "What have you been up to?"

"Nothing," Tom said guiltily.

"Now, young Thomas, I wasn't born yesterday. I can see from that look on your face. Your dad used to look at me just the same."

"What's for lunch?" He asked, knowing this would distract her. Following her into the homely kitchen, he gave Jo a mischievous wink. Being a keen and wonderful cook, Grandma was happy to talk of the home-baked steak and kidney pudding, as he had known she would be.

They chatted to Grandma about the morning's fun and games but no one mentioned the secret place they had found. They had an unspoken agreement and did not discuss it.

After lunch, they played at the back door with Grandma's new tabby kitten, one of her many and various animals. Mum was always saying how ridiculous it was, like a zoo, but Ellie, Tom and Jo loved them all. Mum sent them with books and board games to keep them occupied but these always returned home untouched after the holidays. The enormous garden and animals, including the other three cats, hens, mad terrier and fish in the pond, created such an entertaining, chaotic environment, boredom never came into it!

Little did they realise just how unnecessary any additional amusements would be that summer…

In the hot hazy sunshine, they teased the new kitten, Troubles, with a piece of string. When Tom judged the coast was clear, he showed Ellie and Jo the wound, which was now causing him extreme pain. Still bleeding profusely; he had been unable to stop it and had resorted to a long sleeved T-shirt to conceal it.

Ellie was incensed when she saw the nasty bleeding gash.

"How on earth did you do that?" She had little sympathy for stupidity, especially when Tom's often got them into such trouble! She was certain Grandma would ban them from going over the back if she saw this. Tom was uncertain whether he should tell her the truth because he knew she would not believe him. While he debated, Jo had disappeared to get Grandma's first aid kit from the kitchen cupboard. Fortunately, Grandma was upstairs and Jo was soon running back with it

Ellie was still quizzing Tom. "It was obviously not a fall – that's a bite. But what kind of creature? It looks horrendous."

Tom explained to them what had taken place and just as he suspected, Ellie would not listen. Jo tenderly cleaned the wound and put a neat plaster on it, treating him with care as she would her injured animal friends. Although only nine, she wanted to be a vet when she grew up…or a princess?

"If Tom is lying, where is Scrap, Ellie? We have to find him." She turned to Tom imploringly, "Show me where you left him, Tom?" She would not be put off.

Predictably Ellie did not believe Tom, "I really think we've had enough trouble. Scrap will turn up. It was spooky! I'm not sure its such a great idea to go back there." She was not scared, but as a bright, quick, 12 year old, she sensed danger lurking in the undergrowth. She had been nicknamed "The Thinker," by her dad, Mark, because she would sit and puzzle out solutions to problems, not contenting herself until she had the answer. She often listened to conversations about difficult issues quietly and would subsequently provide an unusually smart conclusion to the problem to the amazement of those around her.

On this occasion, it was an instinctive response and she could not explain why she felt so unnerved. What if Tom was telling the truth? The thick green darkness had made her skin creep and in the dell earlier she had felt a sensation of the green moss covering her feet and enveloping her ankles as though…

Jo interrupted her thoughts. "Mmmm. Know what you mean. It was weird. A secret belonging to the Elves or something." Jo mumbled dreamily. Joanne, her full name, had a lively imagination, living in a world of her own, brimming with princesses and fanciful ideas.

Remembering Scrap though, she stated emphatically, "We have to find Scrap!"

Tom laughed at them, "You're both daft. C'mon lets go. We do have to find Scrap." He ran off making Troubles jump, laughing loudly as he did so. Tom had forgotten the fear he had previously experienced, now full of curiosity and bravado once more.

Jo followed quickly but Ellie trailed reluctantly behind. They could never catch up with him and today was no exception. By the time they had reached the wooden fence at the brow of the hill, he had vanished. It took them ages to rediscover the mossy den. It was so well obscured. When they finally located it and shouted to him there was no response. Over and over, they called him. Nothing.

"What's he up to now?" Ellie muttered irritably. He was always either in trouble, causing trouble or dragging them into it. Neither of the girls wanted to enter. While they hesitated, debating their next move, a huge bat flew past them at speed, from the dark opening; strange looking with a florid red head. A sudden, shimmering, hazy glow around the entrance gave them little opportunity to consider the bat further. They could just visualise Tom's vague outline shifting and indistinct against a brightness that could not be the gloom of the dell behind him.

"Are you coming in? Or what? I can hear Scrap, he's here!" He seemed unaware of what was happening but continued, "It's amazing!"

Jo called Scrap and he reappeared, tail wagging enthusiastically with Tom now outside the entrance once more.

"You looked weird! What happened?" Jo was desperate to know, as was Ellie, although she was more uncertain and concerned.

"I went through the ferns and instead of being in the hidey-hole, I was in a bright kind of tunnel. I felt different, older or something. Scrap was there. Did you see the bat?" He continued excitedly "I don't know but it felt like it's a tunnel leading somewhere. Its like a Secret Club, isn't it?"

Ellie replied sternly, her brow furrowed deeply, "Whatever it is, or was, there's something very strange about that place and I'm not sure any of us should go back in!"

As they set off back to the house, Jo glanced over her shoulder at the entrance to the Secret Club and gasped.

Chapter Two

Gateway To Faerspring

"Wait…What's that?" Jo exclaimed explosively, pointing toward the entrance. It was glistening, like a reflection in a rippling pool of silvery water. As they looked, they could see it gleaming and glowing warm against the stillness of the surrounding cool green ferns. Their eyes were transfixed on the subtle movement and then, abruptly, it stopped; as though it had simply been their imaginations running riot.

Tom, oblivious to danger as usual, moved back into the entrance and found himself in the chilly mossy darkness once more. It was quiet. Jo entered next, expectantly, followed cautiously by Ellie. Staring at each other they reflected in quiet amazement on the sight they had witnessed.

They continued thinking and talking about it long after they had returned to the house. What it meant, what it was, and eventually, after much discussion, whether it had happened at all? It was exciting but scary.

"Shouldn't you be asleep?" Grandma called from the kitchen. But sleep was elusive that night.

"I can't sleep Grandma! Can you bring me a drink?" Jo bellowed back.

Grandma came upstairs, armed with hot chocolate and a digestive biscuit each. She waited quietly until they finished.

"Make sure you clean your teeth after or your mum'll be after me," she said in a conspiratorial whisper.

"Do we have to?" Tom pleaded.

"Yes!" She said firmly. "Now that's enough, young Tom."

He knew arguing would be pointless. Tom gave an unavoidable "ouch" as she hugged him lovingly; regrettably it caused him to flinch as his increasingly painful arm was squeezed unbearably. Ellie and Jo both shot him a warning look.

"What's wrong, Tom?"

"Nothing." He replied.

"Hug me! Hug me!" from Jo and a simultaneous "My turn, Grandma" from Ellie rescued the situation, distracting Grandma from further questions. She gave them both a goodnight kiss and closed the door behind her. They did as they were told and tried to snuggle down to sleep once more.

Tom, despite endless words and descriptions, had been quite unable to convey his earlier experiences and feelings to his sisters. He knew they wouldn't understand and would probably not believe him; it was his own fault, he joked too much.

His mind drifted back as he remembered how he had felt, as though he had become swallowed up in his surroundings for those few brief moments, having new knowledge and exciting thoughts. He lay awake for some time trying to make sense of it all. His arm ached fearfully. He had told Ellie and Jo to say nothing to Grandma; she was such a worrier and would probably forbid them to play up there again. Anyway, there was no point, he'd told them, and it wouldn't do any harm to keep it secret. Sleep long escaped him as he dwelled on where the Secret might take them.

Jo was busy with her own fretful thoughts. Lying awake, she stared up at the yellow floral curtains, as was her habit, in her creative and sensitive way. She liked to imagine animals in the petals and leaves.

Tonight though, she could only think about Tom, he had looked so odd. She was sure he had been wearing different clothes and his face had looked different in those few moments. Eventually she fell asleep next to Ellie, in Grandma's large double bed, stroking the exhausted Scrap who was beside her, twitching as he dreamt of horrifying bats trying to nip him!

Ellie knew Jo had dropped off from her steady rhythmic breathing but so many questions continued tumbling through her head. Why had the entrance shimmered in that bizarre way? Why had Tom been surrounded by light in such a dark hidey-hole? What was it that had bitten him like that? She had seen the enormous bat but it didn't make sense.

Her reputation as a Thinker was well earned that evening. She lay awake considering the endless possibilities. Could there possibly be a passageway to somewhere else? A time tunnel, of sorts? A portal, she thought they were called. Musing, until she finally fell asleep, Ellie dreamt about a tunnel, leading to a world far away in another time with inhabitants who were in need of her help.

On waking next day, Tom's most prominent thought was not breakfast, as was usual for him, but the Secret Club. Had it been a dream? Had he exaggerated the experience in his own mind? It seemed so unreal now, but as he watched Ellie and Jo rouse, the look of anticipation on their excited faces made him acutely aware that it must all have been true.

His arm was stiff and aching. Jo removed the dressing. It had a dreadful black circle around it and smelt foul. She redressed it carefully, having already smuggled the first aid kit upstairs.

Grandma was puzzled by their hurry that morning, but assumed they were keen to get outside to see Troubles. They finished breakfast quickly and ran out into the garden, ignoring Troubles and the other cats lazing peacefully in the early morning sun, they sped on by and flew up the hill. As they neared the fence, their pace slackened and they came to an uneasy standstill a little way from the Secret.

There was a contradictory air of uncertainty and eagerness in the silent pause. Each of them waited for the other to speak. No one did. Instead they walked slowly with deliberation towards the doorway together and then crossed the threshold. The thick, green heaviness clung to them, like a heavy cloak enfolding them. They waited.

Ellie spoke first, "I knew nothing was going to happen. The entrance was still. It's only when it's shimmering that it works!"

Jo challenged her, "How do you know?"

Tom replied instead, "No, she's right. Anyway there's no bat today. It only happens when the bat appears."

"Don't be ridiculous!" Jo persisted arguing, "You don't get bats in daylight. They're nocturnal. I watched…." Jo was always keen to share her extensive knowledge of animals.

Tom was not interested today, in fact he was angry, and interrupted sharply, "Are you saying I'm lying?"

They all fell silent; secretly they were both disappointed and relieved. They waited in the gloom. Jo suddenly said, "Maybe it only happens once in every hundred years! Maybe it will never happen again."

Again, silence, until Ellie asked thoughtfully "Where do you think it would lead us if it were shimmering?"

Jo laughed, "I read a book once about a tunnel that took these people to the centre of the earth."

They fell back into their own thoughts until a crimson headed bat of enormous proportions suddenly flew into the fern cave and out again, as quick as a flash. They jumped up, shocked, and pursued it. When they found themselves out in the open again they searched the sky to see where it had gone, but mysteriously it had evaporated into thin air, and in broad daylight too!

Ellie and Jo were so focused on the elusive bat it was a while before they realised that Tom had also disappeared.

Ellie screamed "Look, Jo! The tunnel…."

Once more the doorway shimmered and shifted, Ellie peered into the entrance. Jo watched in amazement as Ellie's body became hazy, indistinct, her outline glowing with dazzling rainbow colours, her face becoming ghostly emerald green. It reminded Jo of pictures of fairies she had seen in Grandma's old-fashioned storybooks.

Her ears and nose altered shape too, becoming delicately pointed and more sharply defined. Her eyes were bright and sparkling like jewels, the colour of a blue-green deep pool glinting in the sunlight, not her usual grey-blue at all. Jo could not speak and did not know what to do, especially since Ellie seemed to be floating into the shimmering haze with no concern whatsoever. Her arms now appeared thinner and paler, outstretched invitingly toward Jo.

Then astonishingly, two tendrils of translucent rainbow-coloured jelly wrapped sinuously around Jo dragging her into the liquid, shaking void. Silently she too, was swallowed up into the viscous gel.

Revolving and spinning, they all spiralled out of control in the multi-coloured tunnel. Falling, they tumbled over a kaleidoscopic waterfall, into a pool of nothingness. Being pulled downward, they were now surrounded by a clinging, heavy darkness.

The girls had caught up with Tom and the three of them were screaming, but it was soundless, as though the black vacuum sucked in all sound and light. Initially, their bodies felt stretched and taut; then alternately, shrunken and shrivelled. This was associated with an intense tingling in their extremities and faces.

In a flash, the colours returned again, swirling and mingling, until the only shade was a deep, iridescent green. A familiar feeling of floating within another dell possessed them, this was different though, enormous and bottomless.

Instead of a moss carpet below, there was only inky emptiness. Still, no sounds were being emitted from their gaping mouths, but gradually they were able to visualise each other's outlines, with that came relief that they were not alone in this ordeal but were hovering side by side.

Each human face had taken on an ageless quality, with finely pointed ears and delicate, sharp chins. The brother and sisters now shared ethereal, alabaster, almost translucent, skin, perfect without blemish, freckle or wrinkle and curly shoulder length hair, even Tom's usually straight mop had been replaced. Lips were full, bow-shaped, like rosebuds, lying underneath delicately upturned noses. Their well-nourished, chubby limbs had become lithe and thin. Their outer clothes were gone and it was clear their bodies, too, were singularly slender.

Gazing, wide-eyed, at each other, they realised that the transformation they were witnessing was also occurring in them. As they tried to accustom themselves to this, the surroundings underwent another change. The green faded; a thick, clinging mist enveloped them, so overwhelming they could not even see their hands in front of their faces.

Gradually the density lessened and became wispier. The huge dell had disappeared and clouds were speeding past at hundreds of kilometres per hour, like a hurricane. There was a sensation of plunging downwards at speed.

Fear gripped them. Then, without warning their feet came into contact with a solid surface, causing them to crumple in a dishevelled heap.

Chapter Three
The Awakening

Tom felt a peculiar warmth coursing through his cold damp limbs as he surfaced groggily. He looked down and saw his wound had inexplicably healed into a dark scar. The pain had subsided to his great relief. There was little else to feel relieved about though as he gazed at his unfamiliar body.

Ellie and Jo sat up, gasping with shock as they stared around. Afloat on a transparent platform, they found themselves in a huge emerald tinted cavern. A faint green mist swirled overhead in its heights. Far below was a rocky floor.

From the obscuring, dense fog, a figure appeared, arms outstretched like wings. His figure was like theirs and, as he glided towards them, they realised that this apparition was real. He landed gracefully on the platform, immediately in front of them.

"Hi! I'm Methven." He spoke, as though nothing out of the ordinary had just occurred, instead of the mind numbing experience it had actually been.

"You are Emeriel." He pointed at Ellie, "Jenna," pointing at Jo, and "Jes," at Tom. "We are expecting you. Please follow me." It was all so confusingly unreal and made worse by the fact that Methven now had his arms outstretched again and had started to rise from the platform, seeming to expect them to do the same!

"Hold on!" Tom interrupted abruptly. "We aren't who you think we are. You're thinking of someone else."

"Yes," Ellie added, "We've got to be getting back to Grandma's," which, albeit very sensible, was rather optimistic under the circumstances and sounded somewhat desperate.

Methven drew his arms back into his chest and lowered height, landing gently beside them again. He turned toward Ellie smiling, revealing perfectly formed, pearly white teeth.

"I know this is strange and difficult for you," he started kindly. "But we really must go. It's not safe in the Autoporter for long." He glanced around anxiously, reiterating his point. "Time for explanations later." As if to underline his statement, the mist swirling around the cavern roof began to twist and turn ever faster. "Please follow me quickly!"

Tom spotted a few of the vicious, terrifying bats and shouted to Ellie and Jo above the noise, now emanating loudly from the roof, "We've got to go now. Look up there! He's right."

Ellie glanced up and saw the cause of Tom's alarm. She knew he was right, but was feeling very annoyed with him for getting them into this.

Methven called behind him, "Like this…lift your arms."

They soon discovered it was as easy as he made it appear. Effortlessly, they took off behind Methven. They did not know it then but they had received their only lesson in transflight, although perhaps they could have done with a full course. However, on a trial by error process, they soon appreciated that subtle turns of their hands influenced both height and direction.

Initially they careered into each other and the platform but they knew they must keep up with Methven. He shouted a word of command at the wall of the chamber, inaudible against the rushing wind and fast thickening cloud. It caused a green translucent curtain, previously invisible against the cavern wall ahead, to glide slowly open.

The fleeing group disappeared through the opening, which then closed abruptly with an air of finality behind them.

Surrounded by rugged craggy mountaintops they transflighted over passes, shrouded in mist. Deep ravines etched by glorious waterfalls lay far beneath them, similar to the ones back home although much grander. Then, there were tree-like plants, with a completely unfamiliar appearance having gnarled twisted trunks and unusual bearded tendrils. Ellie reflected that they must be enormous if they could be viewed from this height.

However, there was little time for observation or speculation as Methven was taking them nearer the crags and ravines, darting dangerously, he soared and dipped to avoid them. Descending through the mist into a very deep hidden valley, he paused without warning and drew his arms into his chest. A glass platform appeared out of the mist with a strangely engraved edge,

"ϑΥΣΤΙΧΕ ΑΝΔ ΛΙΓΗΤ."

Spectacular vivid colours flashed through it.

They tried to stop as he had done but somehow ended up colliding into one another. Landing sprawled out; they found themselves looking through the platform to the valley hundreds of metres below.

"Whoa!" Tom yelled gazing down in amazement.

There were so many questions waiting to erupt, instead there was an awkward silence as they tried to gather their chaotic thoughts.

Methven seemed to know what they were thinking though and said, "No answers now! There will be time later. For now rest!" This seemed an excellent suggestion. They had discovered that although transflight looked graceful and effortless it was, in fact, quite exhausting. Their bodies felt drained and weary.

They quietly admired the beauty of their surroundings; ethereal and mysterious, glimpsing flocks of unusual flying copper coloured creatures in the distance, set against the backdrop of the rugged, snow-covered mountain peaks. It was a fantastic sight.

"Right!" Methven broke into their thoughts "We'd better go as we don't really want to draw attention to your arrival." The platform vanished into the mist, in much the same manner as it had arrived, that is to say, unexpectedly! The novice fliers were all caught out and dropped several feet before outstretching their arms hurriedly.

Methven spun around laughing, "Oops! Sorry! I forgot you're not used to this yet," and flew sharply downward without another word, although he was still chuckling to himself.

The scenery was impressive. They sped past outcrops of rock covered in light pink, rampant, plants clinging like ivy. Water sprang from rocks and trees, which seemed strangely beautiful, and there were multitudes of rivers and lakes. Mist in abundance, too, snaked through many breathtaking valleys as they flew over. It seemed serene and peaceful in the absence of any mechanical sounds.

"No houses, villages or signs of any inhabitants! How strange?" thought Tom.

"Methven must live somewhere, though," Ellie responded silently and then realised with a shock that neither of them had actually spoken. She could see from the startled expression on Tom's face that he had 'heard' her reply.

Methven interrupted her thoughts, although uttered no speech, "You've discovered another ability. Well, a Gifft, as we know it here, really. Thought speech. I will tell you more later. Please hurry!"

Ellie was brought abruptly back to the task in hand, as she almost struck an exceptionally tall tree growing on a jutting crag. Transflight required rather more concentration than she had realised. They continued on for miles; valleys and lakes disappearing rapidly behind them. As the light faded from the sky a dark blue azure glow spread from behind them.

In the distance was a bright green light camouflaged in leaves and foliage. It was at the far end of yet another deep valley, a rushing river disappeared in and out of rocky tunnels, cascading powerfully over waterfalls. The emerald glow increased in intensity as they flew close to the valley floor and as daylight faded it became obvious that this diffuse, dim light was their destination.

Chapter Four
Welhspring

As they approached the strange illumination they saw a vast transparent crystal structure. Gnarled trees wove roots and branches through it, making it seem alive. The trees appeared to be the framework around which the glowing opalescent building had grown. They had never seen anything so beautiful or exquisite. Balanced precariously but elegantly against the rugged, densely wooded hillside, it was high above the valley floor. The green phosphorescence emanated from the fading sunlight, reflecting off the foliage and radiating through the many tiers of crystal within.

Concentration was vital in order to follow Methven swooping low over the scintillating peaks and sinuous branches protruding from the crystal village. He glided slowly to a halt above the highest point and then stepped onto a platform, which simply materialised beneath him. Likewise they halted, with considerable relief, exhausted from their strenuous efforts. It was not with Methven's graceful skill though. Jo bumped into Ellie, causing them both to sprawl across the glass. They gazed in wonder through the multiple levels to an azure river below, with streams branching off, winding its way inextricably amongst the greenery and rainbow lights.

Ellie tried to stand and became aware of a softness and warmth as her hand touched the platform. It could not be glass or crystal, that was obvious, and it radiated peace, which struck Ellie as a ridiculous notion, since solids cannot transmit feelings.

"You are very quick and intuitive, Emeriel," she heard as Methven read her thoughts.

"I'm not Emeriel! And tell me how do you know what I'm thinking?" she flashed back at him.

"It's a Gifft with which only certain Faeries are blessed. You are blessed."

Ellie was beginning to get really annoyed. They had done precisely as they had been told and here they were, with no idea of where…why…or what was happening. Even her thoughts were not her own and her name was not Emeriel!

"You are correct as always, Emeriel," Methven responded audibly, so that Jo and Tom could hear, although, of course, they had no idea what Methven meant. "If you could be patient for just a little longer and follow me. I will explain. Your queries will have answers," he continued, sounding understanding and kindly. "But first you must rest and refresh yourselves."

Yet again, they set off behind Methven. This time, fortunately, on foot. The gleaming transparent surfaces, waterfalls and streams, behind and below, caused dazzling vibrant beams of light to shoot out in multitudinous directions. Strangely though, they began to notice as they glanced around in awe, that the light source was the trailing foliage, suspended along the ceilings of the glassy corridors. The verdant glow permeated all that was visible.

Methven headed down a level and they continued behind him, but not down steps. He stood at the top of a knotted branch, interweaving through the crystal edifice, and gliding gracefully descended to another floor. One by one, they followed him down several branch escalators, becoming quite expert, although Jo had a couple of close shaves, careering out of control and descending one or two awkwardly on her backside. And, of course, Tom could not resist attempting to ascend one or two, to Methven's quiet amusement.

They reached a level with water rippling along in channels in the floor and cascading by the wooden escalators in waterfalls. The water was the deepest clear blue they had ever seen. As they descended further, they noticed more and more water, with trailing leafy ivy-like plants on the ceilings and ferns lining the walls. Underfoot was an ever-thickening carpet of moss and it became difficult to see through the structure despite its transparency. The botanical corridors led to spacious rooms at intersections with either a pool or burbling spring surrounded by smooth rocks and glistening marble of unimaginable shades.

It was all so unreal and unusual, yet there was also a familiarity about it that Ellie could not explain. She felt no fear, rather, a tremendous sense of tranquillity, warmth and an inexplicable unity with this environment.

Finally, they reached the lowest point of the structure and were looking at a rocky cliff face ahead and the valley floor below. A flat slate surface in the cliff glided noiselessly open into the rock as Methven approached, revealing another hidden entrance.

"You will find rest and peace in here," Methven said quietly. "I will send you a Companie to bring you food and fresh clothes." He waved his arm invitingly toward the room. Then, he spun around and was gone. He had disappeared but the three were so astonished at the sight before them they had not noticed.

The room had a transparent ceiling of multifaceted crystal, with water in a thin stream rippling over it. Brightly lit by a couple of foliage lights in the centre of this perfect hexagonal space, the walls were draped, floor to ceiling, in a woven silk fabric made of the finest silver thread, as thin as a spider's web but closely knit. It was about five times the size of Grandma's largest bedroom, massive, with five different levels connected by mini wooden escalators. In the centre of the room was an intricately carved fountain with a golden surround. Unlike everything else they had seen, it was hand crafted rather than having an appearance of being alive.

Jo spoke first, breaking the silence, "Look! Just pinch me and then we can all wake up in Grandma's bed and forget this weird dream… Or do I mean nightmare?"

"It's neither! It's the most fantastic adventure we've ever had!" Tom said, sliding up and down the escalators, enthusiastically.

Ellie fixed him with a look of utter disbelief, "How can you say that? You don't know where we are or why. Adventures can be dangerous! You should know better at your age…"

Tom continued sliding and inadvertently made a discovery, silencing Ellie, fortunately for him. If he waved his hand at waist level to the left at the bottom of the escalator a pedestal would rise from the floor. The three of them investigated and found that this applied to each of three connecting escalators. Ellie explored further. However the revelation that followed made even Tom alarmed.

Chapter Five
Transobjection

As Ellie gently touched the crystal sphere adorning the top of the pedestal, a hammock made from gold thread materialised from the wall. Tom, not to be left out, touched the crystal on the pedestal next to him and another hammock appeared. Jo followed suit. They were shocked to witness a silver and gold panel appearing on the walls above the three hammocks with the words Emeriel, Jes and Jenna in strange lettering.

"That's what Methven keeps calling us," Ellie said, shaking her head, apprehensive at the possible implications. Tom, by contrast, had characteristically already recovered from his fright and was dashing around the room searching for, and finding, other pedestals, resulting in Jo bumping into objects not there previously, to his great delight.

Ellie looked on with increasing disquiet as he brought three magnificent silver armchairs into view with the initials E, J and J embroidered in the strange script.

Jo asked quite sensibly, "Well, how do we know which is yours and which is mine?"

"Easy!" said Tom as the chairs swung around to reveal their portraits, exquisitely but unnervingly fashioned on the back of each. Ellie looked on aghast as she realised that the chairs had turned but Tom had not moved.

"How did you do that?" she queried, nervously.

Tom looked at her, shrugging his shoulders, but, with an impish grin, glanced at the chairs anew as they swung back again.

Ellie fell silent. Jo and Tom found additional pedestals, which brought forth a table and controlled the silver drapes and curtains. Ellie grappled with the fact that although Tom was leaping about engineering all this, he could just, in fact, sit down and cause it to happen. She decided, however, that it might not be prudent to point this out.

The curtain, opposite the door, drew back revealing a panoramic window and although it was now dark outside they could see a blue full moon above the crags stretching out to the right, and an orange crescent-shaped moon, rising to the left.

"Oh my God!" gasped Tom, shocked to the core.

"Tom!" Ellie and Jo chided, automatically with the synchronicity they reserved for such occasions. "You know Grandma doesn't like you saying that," Ellie went on sternly.

"Yes, Yes! B…b…but…." He stammered and spluttered. "Ddd…Don't you realise what this means? We are on another world!"

Jo dissolved into tears. "I want to go home!" She wailed. "I want Grandma!"

Staring at the vista before them the enormity of the situation dawned on them. Ellie spoke first. "The tunnel must have been a vortex or a black hole."

While they were pondering Ellie's suggestion, they heard a faint tinkling noise, like a tiny bell, and a face appeared above one of the two remaining pedestals. The face announced itself, which was somewhat alarming, "My name is Gerianne. I'm your Companie. May I help you?"

Despite their recent revelation, or was it because of it and the fact they had nothing to lose, they jointly replied with an emphatic "Yes!" At which, the face embodied itself to a one metre high slender Faerie similar to Methven but smaller and wearing a white robe and a green belt of thick woven twine, typical Companie garb.

"Are you real?" Jo asked, rather impolitely, curiosity overcoming her.

He nodded, smiling at her, "Methven has sent me to help you. I'm to make sure you have all you need. He said you would be full of questions but were not to worry."

He bustled around the room putting away the chairs, closing the silver curtains and leaving the hammocks, operating the pedestal controls swiftly and efficiently. As they watched they discovered the function of the remaining pedestal. A gold web enclosed the three hammocks, simultaneously filling them with the softest looking down.

"Rest awhile and you will be refreshed." He motioned towards the inviting beds, soft nightgowns were laid out, and they quickly changed, lying down, exhaustion dismissing any possible argument.

A feeling of warmth and contentment filled their minds as their weary bodies responded to the mattress, which enveloped them, making a cosy covering also. In a matter of seconds, only their newly acquired Faerie faces could be seen above the snowy white down. Their long curly lashes fluttered across their sleepy closing eyes.

Waking up the next day was disconcerting. Tom roused first, startled as he glanced around and then caught sight of his hands with their long, elegant fingers and the faint green hue of his skin. He squeezed his eyes speedily shut and re-opened them. "I'm dreaming," he thought hopefully.

"Nooo! You're not!" Ellie said emphatically. It came flooding back to him, like a tidal wave.

"How can you do that?" Tom replied, aloud this time.

"I don't have a clue. But ever since we've come through the tunnel I've known what you are both thinking and there are times when I'd really rather not. Not know, that is."

"Sorry-eee!" muttered Tom, although he wasn't sure if he really was or, even, should be.

Jo was still dozing peacefully which was just as well, since she was the one who most needed her sleep and least needed to hear the conversation, as Ellie well knew from Jo's rather frightened thoughts yesterday.

"Well I think it's great. Imagine how much fun you could have at school. Think of it, Ellie, if you knew what the teachers were thinking you'd be top of the class and you'd be able to pull some great stunts on folk you don't like!"

Ellie wasn't so sure, "Yes but what if you knew when you're friends were thinking bad thoughts about you? Or if you knew something bad was about to happen to someone else because you'd read someone else's evil thoughts?"

They both fell silent, even Tom could see it might have its downside.

Then Tom, ever ready for more fun, said inquisitively, "I wonder what's going on out there?" He focused on the pedestals and the silver curtain, "Can you remember which does what?"

He proceeded to inadvertently operate beds and chairs, using thought alone, resulting in their chaotic appearance and disappearance, in his effort to open the curtain.

Ellie mused about labelling the pedestals, to avoid future confusion and watched as Jo awoke, dazed and mystified, rubbing her eyes in a futile effort to make it all vanish.

Tom, finally, located the pedestal for the curtain and early morning light flooded into the room along with a panorama that made them gasp in a combination of appreciation and apprehension.

Chapter Six

A New Dawn

The sky, before them, held two huge yellow suns, one of which had a green tinged halo. They stared, unblinking, at the sky and then at the lake, which filled the valley below with deep dark blue water, sparkling like sapphire.

"Why didn't we notice the two suns yesterday?" Jo asked in surprise.

"Because it was cloudy." Emeriel replied, in a matter of fact tone.

A couple of enormous purple-headed birds, the size of ostriches, flitted past in the background. It was awesome, but thought provoking, as everything was so different. The mountains on the far side of the valley were taller and craggier than anything else they had ever known. Time passed.

Tears trickled slowly down Jo's face, as once again she realised how far away she was from home and family. Then, as they looked on the strange scene, there was a sudden movement near the glittering lake and a flock of dark six-legged creatures rushed along the valley floor by the river until they reached the lake edge.

Disappearing in a flash into the lake, these strange animals left barely a trace of a ripple on the water. The disbelieving group continued to watch, anticipating the reappearance but there was nothing to even indicate their existence.

They were, still silently, watching when the bell rang and Gerianne's face appeared behind them. "May I be of service?"

They did not need to be asked twice and despite their disquiet that morning, he received an enthusiastic, "Yes!" from them all.

Tom wasted no time and took the lead; his tummy being the emptiest as usual. "Please may we have some breakfast?"

"Pelfirst? Jes." Gerianne corrected him.

Tom had no idea what he meant and still wondered why Gerianne insisted on calling him 'Jes,' but nodded replying, "If that's food? Yes, please!"

Gerianne appeared in his full form and busied himself around the room. Ellie couldn't help wondering why he didn't use some of his 'Giffts' to sort the place out, and do it with a wave of the hand, rather than the labour-intensive scuttling around with the pedestals.

Gerianne replied to her unasked question silently, "Methven is joining you for pelfirst and some of your questions will be answered then, Emeriel." She could not hear any further thoughts from Gerianne and realised that, as well as the ability to know thoughts, there must be another ability, which prevented one's thoughts from being known, and clearly both Gerianne, and also Methven, must have this Gifft.

Nevertheless, the room was tidied and the table and chairs prepared. There was a central well in the table, with three smaller wells adjacent to each chair. A sapphire crystal button next to the central well brought forth an additional well and chair if pressed once. Pressing it a further time caused the central well to be filled with plants and berries. Hexagonal biscuits, soft in texture, simultaneously appeared in each of the place wells.

Gerianne elevated himself slightly, inclined his head and was gone.

Tom and Jo were looking quizzically at the fourth place well; when Methven's friendly smiling face appeared above it.

"May I join you?"

Ellie, the least surprised, responded first. "Of course!" She replied keenly.

He gave her an understanding look and she remembered he was party to her thoughts. She would like to be able to put a block on this intrusion.

"All in good time."

She knew his reply and felt annoyed, but he continued smiling amiably.

"Please let's start. Let me help you, Jenna." He indicated the food and pressed a sapphire crystal button at the side of Jo's well, a share of the food was transported through the air into the well. Tom did not wait to be served but pressed his crystal immediately.

It was curious to see food in transflight but this was only an insignificant consideration, in the face of such nagging hunger. Ellie had more grace and poise and, whilst she too was starving, she allowed Methven to serve her, and gave Tom a suitably disapproving look for his lack of manners.

Methven started. The leaves were an unusual spiky triangular shape and were mainly purple and blue, with a few more acceptable green colours. He began to explain the various properties of the herbs to them, as they ate eagerly:

Milkworrit; a pale green ivy-shaped leaf with a white tip, for memory improvement and to enhance thought speaking Giffts.

Caldishel; a purple cylindrical leaf, curving in on itself, with a bright red stem, for sharpening listening skills and thought blocking Giffts. (Ellie decided she would perhaps ask for an extra helping of this at an appropriate juncture!)

Thistleberry; a spiky, shiny holly-like leaf with a pale blue hue, for peace and friendship.

Then, there were the berries and fruit:

The Thistleberry itself; which was an even paler blue than its leaf, translucent, spherical cherry-size and eaten to provide courage. (Sounds ominous, thought Ellie as she listened to Methven's guide to the local menu.)

Duckberry; a dark green berry with a hairy surface about the size and shape of an almond, for transflight and clear vision.

Broomiefiel; a large, dark brown fruit, grapefruit size, but so shiny it glistened, apparently for truth and honesty.

Then there was also the hexagonal biscuit, Crillis; vital for life as Methven explained and an essential ingredient in the diet, for energy. The specially appointed Crillis makers of Faerspring prepared it.

Ellie interrupted the monologue and asked,

"Is that where we are? Faerspring?"

Methven replied smiling, "You are in Welhspring, on the Island of Faerspring, Emeriel. But please, you must eat or you will weaken and you need your strength. I will explain as we eat."

So began their first meal on Faerspring.

"Will we get more pelfirst later?" Tom enquired hopefully, tucking in eagerly.

"No, Jes." Methven laughed. "But, you will have pelevemel though and we usually have a snack at midpel, pellun." Tom was greatly relieved to hear this. They were so busy eating none of them thought to confirm what midpel was but had rather accepted it as being midday.

The berries and leaves were so refreshing and mouth watering they were sorry there were not more but the Crillis, although of small quantity, was extremely satisfying. Traditionally left until towards the end of the meal, it tasted like the sweetest shortbread, melting quickly on the tongue and leaving a tingle after, followed by a radiance spreading throughout their bodies. Ellie felt sure it had enhanced their new features.

Methven looked at her and she heard his thought.

"You are right as usual, Emeriel. Traditional Faerie food enhances our features and Giffts, some of which you have already discovered."

"Wow!" Interrupted Jo, inadvertently, "Is there any more Crisylys?"

"Crillis, Jenna." Methven frowned briefly, an unusual event but there was a good reason for this, as they later found out. "I'm afraid that is not possible but I am glad you enjoyed it."

Drinks were taken at the end of the meal when another crystal platform appeared, floating near the window, with four golden goblets inlaid with gems of multi-colours and shapes. Jo, who loved pretty things, studied them closely.

Ellie was much more interested in the green vapour, which they were emitting. Tom was only interested in drinking and was rising to go over and pick up a goblet, having forgotten his Gifft but Methven transobjected them to the table, chuckling.

"Emerene." He said grandly as Tom hurriedly sat down again. "A special recipe, known only to the Council of Welhspring."

Ellie, not to be distracted further at this stage, began to ask some of the many questions, which were troubling her, "Methven, please can you tell us what other Giffts exist and why are we known by different names here?" She enquired quietly, with determination.

He nodded, understanding her need to know. "Transflight you have experienced already, almost all Faeries have this ability. Thought speech is another Gifft, bestowed only on certain Faeries, and also rarely in the other races, to special individuals, on Faerspring. It is usually Giffted for a very specific purpose and is considered exceptional. Thought blocking is partly Gifft, partly ability, which those who have the Gifft of thought speech, can develop in time and of necessity. There are others also but it is essential that you realise that we consider them precious and are to be used only for the common good." He paused reflectively, considering whether he should say anymore at this stage but Jo was fiddling with her goblet and Tom was still looking hungrily around for more food.

"For the moment Emeriel, I will say no more except that you are aware that Jes has the Gifft of transobjection, and Jenna has another special Gifft. Both will be required. You are here for a purpose. Justice does not Gifft Faeries lightly." Once again, only Ellie was privy to his thoughts, albeit briefly.

"More berries, Jes?" Gerianne appeared unexpectedly and Ellie knew Methven had summoned him. Jes nodded relieved to have been asked.

"Please could I have one or two more Caldishel leaves, Gerianne?" Emeriel asked politely. Gerianne served her, willingly.

"Gerianne, please would you prepare our guests to meet the Princess at midpel?" Methven smiled at them continuing, "She is honoured to have you here and wishes to meet you as soon as possible," with that, he was gone.

Jo's ears picked up at this; she was keen to meet a Princess and most curious. Her favourite game at Grandma's was dressing up and she always wanted to be the Princess.

Gerianne busied himself again, tables, chairs, goblets and assorted furniture disappearing neatly into its appointed place.

Tom hunted around desperately for his trainers, his favourite comfy old ones, which was not an unusual pursuit for him in the mornings. Grandma used to joke about the way his trainers and clothes vanished. On this occasion though, Ellie and Jo's clothes and footwear were also missing and Gerianne produced garments from a concealed closet although quite how he had opened it was a mystery to Ellie who was scrutinising his movements closely. Even knowing where it was, she could neither see it, nor knew how it was opened. She made a mental note to watch him even more closely next time and wondered if he had triggered it by thought, in some way.

They were each given a pale green, knee-length robe of finest velvet with a silver, platted belt and dark green soft leather shoes which were pointed at the ends. Ellie recalled a pair of Grandma's shoes called 'winkle pickers', pointed like these. Grandma had said they were extremely uncomfortable; by contrast these were light and flat, like walking in bare feet so soft was the hide. They were a perfect fit, as were the robes, which was really quite alarming when Ellie considered it.

Gerianne handed each a garland of fine silver, interwoven with deep green foliage for their hair.

Tom looked at this and both Ellie and Gerianne heard his thought, "If they think I'm wearing that they'd better think again!"

Gerianne spoke firmly, before Ellie had a chance to reproach him for his rudeness, "Jes, the Princess will expect this. It is a sign of respect."

Tom acquiesced which was surprising but Ellie caught another thought momentarily, as he turned to take it from Gerianne. "Once. Maybe, but that's it!" She knew Gerianne had caught it too, as the corners of his mouth were twitching faintly.

Ellie and Jo's had faint tiny blue blooms, also entwined, distinguishing them from his, but this was lost on the sulking Tom.

As soon as they placed them on, the most peculiar sensation occurred.

Chapter Seven

Zithanduel

Jo looked across at Ellie as an absurd indescribable sensation of change filled her head and a thick white haze swamped her thoughts. She felt an unknown blood surge through her pulsing veins. Instead of seeing her brother and sister simply appearing different, she now saw Emeriel and Jes gazing back at her in their traditional Faerspring dress, having undergone the same transformation with the same new found knowledge.

They set off confidently, with an air of those who belong, toward the Great Welhspring Hall, a place of prestige and importance in the Faerspring world. Confusion had been replaced with acceptance, though many questions remained. Each understood they were now Emeriel, Jes and Jenna.

Situated on the uppermost level of the vast crystal citadel, the Hall was filled with brilliant light from the two suns and flashes of rainbow colour radiated from the many aspects of the complex ceiling. The floor was of snowy white stone. Six circular pools of water, connected by channels were situated around the perimeter of the hexagonal shaped Hall with silver and foliage decorated bridges making spectacular footpaths across. The central portion of the Hall was a perfect circle with a terrace of transparent seats, each with a silver cushion. The effect was stunning and those who saw it for the first time were overawed. There was a central dais, raised above the centre, unsupported and hovering silently.

The Hall bustled with the inhabitants of Welhspring and guests, their appearance and dress now accepted as normal by Emeriel, Jes and Jenna. Since their transformation, there was a new familiarity about the Faerspring way of life.

An observant outsider from Earth would have noticed a number of unusual aspects to the scene below though. There were no children and all were of the same slender build. Groups of twos and threes nodded together, engaged in conversation, but not always using speech. Also, peculiarly, the water flowing around the room clearly flouted the law of gravity. But, Emeriel, Jes and Jenna looked on the vista with interest but much that a visitor would find odd, now seemed perfectly ordinary to them, and so, as the second sun ascended in the sky with its green aura as it always did, it went unnoticed by them.

Their attention was fixed on a panel, in the glittering roof, sliding silently aside allowing a bright shaft of light to illuminate the dais, a spectrum of colour dancing and sparkling around. A figure appeared descending vertically in graceful transflight onto the dais. Whilst she was noticeably younger looking than the audience, her presence filled the Hall. Blonde curls cascaded around her thin delicate faerie-like face and Jenna could not help thinking she had never seen anyone more lovely. Her fragile frame was wrapped in glistening gold robes, with a matching garland and soft golden shoes. Her eyes were a piercing bright blue but her smile was warm and dazzling and Emeriel knew she was to be trusted, though how she could not have explained.

The Princess sat lightly on the gold cushioned dais and was greeted with Faerspring homage, the assembly transfiguring a metre or so in the air and bowing low at the hips. They began singing in clear, sweet, melodic high-pitched voices:

"All shared, all belong,

All important, all live.

Long live the Princess,

Long live Faerspring,

In the name of Justice,

Forever."

It was such a simple refrain, yet sung with utmost reverence and deep emotion.

The Princess addressed the inhabitants:

"My people, I thank you, for your respect and your presence. You are good citizens. My thanks, also, to the representatives of Elhspring and Silhspring, I know you have travelled far to be here.

"I have called this special meeting of the Gathring to announce the arrival of those foretold in the Ancient Book of the Flowers and Lore of Faerspring. I entreat you to make them feel most welcome and accepted, for we know they will rescue us from our plight, as prophesied, and we will be grateful.

"I will meet with the Elders of the Gathring to make plans, which will enable the Chosen to fulfil all that is expected. Their arrival is indicative that the Time is close at hand. Before we send them out, there will be a celebration, in their honour, and we will introduce them formally and equip them for their journey.

"That is all, for now. Justice be with Faerspring!" She finished with the ceremonial blessing.

The assembled citizens elevated a metre and bowed, a strange but hallowed sight.

Emeriel, Jes and Jenna had participated in this ceremony in an almost trance-like state, knowing unquestioningly that the Princess was referring to them as the Chosen Ones and accepting the rituals as though they had never known any other world.

The garlands had changed their understanding of their position in Faerspring and they had a newfound knowledge of Faerspring tradition and procedure although their characters remained unaltered. It was as though they had come to visit from another part of Faerspring rather than another far away world.

Jes whispered to Emeriel, "Ok! So what was all that about?"

Emeriel replied quietly, "I'm beginning to realise, the garland has made me see. I'm Emeriel here and Ellie on earth. I know that we're going to have a hard task."

Jenna said, "I feel the same and I'm scared. What does it all mean?"

Jes shook his head regretfully, "All I know is, I look at you and I see Emeriel and Jenna. That tunnel has got us into much deeper trouble than I ever imagined!"

The ceremony over, they left the Hall, transflighting with ease without a moment's consideration, escorted by Gerianne. There were many Faerspringians in the crystal corridors, seated by pools or gliding along smiling at them in welcome, as they passed.

Gerianne felt conscious of their need for some relaxation and time to reflect on all that had occurred. He made a silent suggestion to Emeriel.

"Would you like to follow me to the Glade of Gillilien. It might be restful. We often go there when we need to think and there is a wonderful view of the Timewatcher's Tower in the distance!"

Chapter Eight

The Timewatcher's Tower

The Ancient Book of Lore and Flowers of Faerspring was kept safely locked away, in the Timewatcher's Tower, which was located high on a hillside many Faermills away from Welhspring. In clear weather, Welhspring was visible to the naked eye and with the correct apparatus, that is the Lens of Myreellien, it was just possible to see Elhspring and Silhspring several hundred Faermills away.

Jasper was perched on the elaborately carved wooden seat, in the middle of the Lookover. Slim with curling blonde shoulder length hair tumbling over his purple velvet tunic, his keen blue-purple eyes scanned the horizon for telltale signals, which would indicate the arrival of the much feared and equally hated Devlins.

He was bored with this most highly respected task. His Master had repeatedly tried to impress upon him the importance and worthiness of his duty but he had never seen a Devlin yet. He had been told the Lore of Faerspring many times in the fifty yers he had watched, and he wondered exactly what he might really do if he ever actually saw one of the 'Dreaded Race', as they were often referred to. Many were afraid of using the word, "Devlin", for fear of inadvertently summoning them. Superstition and nonsense, his master said, but Jasper was not so sure.

"Report forthwith to the Timewatcher, whereupon the Timewatcher will inform the Princess without delay." Jasper repeated the Lore to himself, without thought. He had decided many moons ago, though, if he ever viewed the Dreaded Race approaching over a distant hill, it would take all he could not to simply run for his life, never mind the "Report forthwith…."

The Lore foretold of this Race from another world, which had only one dim blue sun. Jasper had always found it impossible to believe that another world, with only one sun, could exist but if the Lore said they lived in darkness underground, then it must surely be.

Then there was the supporting Lore and history of the other races on Faerspring, the Ilves. They also believed that, once many, many, many generations before, the Dreaded Race had been Faeries also but had been banished. The Ilve History described them as having black eyes with a hidden extra eye behind their left ear. It was rumoured this was for locating food at a distance of two Faermills. Not so much of an ear as a nose, Jasper had thought when he had learned this. Their skin was reported to be of the toughest hide, wrinkly and very rough but hairless. The Ilves feared them because of their dark powers.

Jasper gazed at the distant horizon, thinking about the Tales the Timewatcher had told him in many of the long, dark nights of story telling. Jasper was tall for one of Faerspring origin and the Timewatcher had told him he would be glad of it if he ever had to fight a Devlin. This was little comfort though as the Timewatcher had elaborated on the evil deeds committed on the other races of Faerspring by the Devlins and he knew they would be fearful adversaries, caring for no one and nothing.

Jasper began to fidget restlessly, numbness spread across his haunches as he perched on his seat. He knew he still had a whole pel to watch before nelfall; he had been up from before pellight. Although his task often became boring, it never made him careless and his watchful eyes continued scanning the horizon. The Timewatcher had lectured him too many times to allow any hint of slackness to creep in. One pel, unexpectedly, he knew that he would be the one to alert the World of Faerspring to the doom-laden return of the Dreaded Race.

Jasper's formal title was the Bud Keeper and as such it was his responsibility to maintain and water the Lilly of Faerspring, which was kept carefully locked away in the Garden Room, on the roof of the Timewatchers Tower. Early before pellight, he would arise and immediately set about tending the Lilly. At pellight, a new petal would begin to unfurl and this marked the beginning of a new pel. He then had to resume his other task of Looking Out. After 25 pels a new bud would form and be tenderly transplanted, indicating the beginning of a new Lilly plant and a new fler. There would be ten Lilly Plants and therefore ten flers in a yer, each as well tended and perfect as the last.

Next yer was to be the Yer of the Faerspring Rose and last had been the Yer of the Rall Tulp, which Jasper had found particularly tiresome. It had proved extremely difficult to recognise a new bud appearing on such a minute plant. However since there were always 25 pels in a fler with the eye of faith, knowledge of tradition and, of course, precise caring and maintenance, somehow he had managed.

An outsider might have wondered about the relevance of all this, especially considering Faerspring was so controlled by meal times and the rising of the two suns. Time watching, though, was an honoured custom and of utmost importance. Strangers were informed, many a time, of the Yer of the Rock Rose, which was kept by a lazy Bud-Keeper and had disastrous consequences. Ceremonies were missed, meals were late and the all-important Festival of Spring was omitted altogether. It was even said that the Bud-Keeper had let the plant die and a new one had to be found by an exceedingly angry Timewatcher. Needless to say the Bud-Keeper was sent away to the desert lands beyond Silhspring where it was rumoured he tended the prickly Prucklemouth Grippes, used to make the much-loved Gripple Juice. It was a favourite of many of the Faerspring races especially the Silherners but harvesting and tending the Grippes was a difficult and unpleasant task, of course.

In addition to the Bud Keeper, the Timewatcher had another assistant, the Lore Keeper. Both were subject to the stern discipline imposed by the Timewatcher. This particular pellight, Jish was dusting each page of the Lore respectfully and thoroughly, whilst humming one of his favourite Faerspring odes, as was his wont.

"ϑοψ το τηε Λορε,

ϑοψ το τηε πελ,

ϑοψ το τηε Νορ,

ϑοψ το τηε ωελλ."

Jish continued turning the pages with his slender fingers. He was frail in his stature, even for a Faerspringian, and had rich dark curls tumbling over deep velvety purple eyes. His face regularly held a mischievous smile. Younger than Jasper, he was dressed in his usual black cloak; appropriate to his title edged with the words,

Λορε Κεεπερ ανδ Σερϖαντ οφ Φαερσπριγ,

worn over a pair of tight blue leggings with soft dark blue leather shoes.

The Timewatcher rustled into the Hall, swift and sour as ever. He was a strange sight unless you witnessed him each pel, as Jasper and Jish did. He had a dark purple velvet cloak edged with black and gold trim interwoven intricately with a design from the Lore,

Τιμε ωιλλ νοτ ωαιτ εξχεπτ φορ ϑυστιχε

repeated around it and a belt in the same colours with

Τρυτη ανδ τιμε βελονγ το ϑυστιχε

written on it. The most remarkable thing about the cloak was its transparency; through it one could see nothing except what lay beyond.

Jish looked up at the bearded face, with the unsmiling black beady eyes staring moodily back at him, and prudently he stopped singing before the Timewatcher could scold him for it! The Timewatcher frowned, speaking in the tongue of the Lore

”Τηε Χηοσεν Ονεσ αρε ηερε.”

Jish already knew that the Chosen Ones had arrived. Jasper had told him earlier. He knew the Lore foretold that he and Jasper were soon to meet them. As Lore Keeper, Jish knew as much of the Lore as the Timewatcher himself; only Princess Zithanduel, also the High Chieftanna of Welhspring, and her sisters knew more of the pages in other ancient languages and even they could not know the Lore that was yet to become clear. There were over two thousand, dust covered, leather bound pages to it and much of it had yet to be revealed. Jish knew every word of the Faerspringian portion, which was well over six hundred pages, only a little to do with the fact that he had to dust every single page pelly!

It took all pel, too, he thought ruefully. Each peleve though, the Timewatcher imparted more understanding of the Lore and Jish, ever keen to learn, knew that in time he would be the next Timewatcher, although he had only been Lore Keeper for some two hundred yers. The Timewatcher had been inexperienced, at four hundred yers old, when he had been promoted from Lore Keeper. Even as a young Lore Keeper he had been stern and grumpy. It was rumoured in Faerspring that he had been disappointed not to be the Bud Keeper, as he would then have become the Wise One of Faerspring and adviser to Zithanduel as Jasper would be.

Either way, Jish looked forward to the pel when he would be the Timewatcher and felt honoured to be in training for such a worthy position. He had resolved to become a fair-minded and kindly teacher to the next Lore and Bud Keeper, so they would not have to endure what he and Jasper had. Before that time came though, he dreamt of overthrowing the Dreaded Race and restoring harmony to his world.

He knew the Lore taught of the brave, kindly Lore Keeper who, together with the Bud Keeper, helped defeat the Devlins. He had repeatedly attempted to ask the Timewatcher about the references to it in other languages but the Timewatcher had simply said, "The time is not yet! On with your chores."

And so it was that, on the pel the Chosen Ones arrived, Jish was unaware of the epic adventure upon which he was about to embark or of his part in it.

Jish continued dusting diligently, glancing up as Jasper glided into the room. He could see Jasper through the Timewatcher's robes and knew that his appearance signalled pelfirst, which would be taken in silence watching the horizon from the Balcony of the Lore Hall.

They sat down at the grand table; white gossamer drapes flapping in the breeze, providing the only sound throughout the meal, which consisted of Thistleberry stew and Duckberry Tea.

After pelfirst, Twit, as Jasper and Jish privately referred to the Timewatcher, would leave to give the sacred Ritual of his Pelly Affirmation to Princess Zithanduel that both the Lore and Time were safe and that the Lilly was flourishing accordingly.

For Jasper and Jish it was their only free time. Twit, being fanatical about time, would be back at midpel precisely and in his absence they had chores and Giffts to develop appropriate to their status, but it was freedom all the same, without Twit's miserable eagle eye upon them.

Topel was no different from any other pel. Twit transfigured to go and meet Zithanduel and they jumped up, dashing to put their wooden chairs beside 'Twit's throne' as they disrespectfully referred to his chair. At a furious pace they swept and tidied the Lore Hall.

Everything had it's home in the Tower; the Bud Trimmer, the Watering Vessel and the Ancient Nutrient Potion, the recipe (known only to the Ilvwood Chief, Gerelf). Jasper and Jish dashed around setting each piece in its precise place so that Twit could not fault them when he returned. They polished and cleaned the Tower's three floors from top to bottom, leaving the five hundred stone steps to the first floor as they were rarely used, and transflight being in use for rituals and permitted in their important roles. They worked as fast as they could at the tiresome tasks, knowing that Twit would return in only a quartpel and they had urgent plans of their own.

They raced up the three flights of tortuous wooden stairs to the ramparts at the top of the Lookover. The beautifully carved wooden seat there was large enough for them both and they were keen to start their favourite game, 'Count the Zellifer', an ancient game, long forgotten in the rest of Faerspring, but it was one of the best aspects of the Keeper's lives. Without their game or their abiding friendship they could not have survived the strict regime. Twit had no idea, of course.

The swift, galloping zellifer were hard to spot due to their green-yellow stripes and characteristic disappearing trick; an innate ability resulting from their need to escape their fearsome predator the tyranghelli. The talent lent great intrigue to the game though and in order for a zellifer to count Jasper and Jish had to be able to see it for two full repetitions of the Faerspring anthem.

Regretfully they virtually always disappeared during the first repetition. Scores were generally low. Jish, out of frustration, on one occasion suggested they play 'Count the Tyranghelli' since there were so many more of them and they did not disappear. This had proved boring in the extreme, as they could not count the winged copper colour creatures, flocking in the skies surrounding the Tower, quickly enough, and scores were then ridiculously high.

Naturally, whilst they played this game, Jasper remained on the lookout for Devlins as always. Even so, when Jasper leapt up suddenly, sending Jish and their seat flying, shouting, "What was that? Did you see?" It was still a dreadful shock to him.

"Hey! It's ma turn," Jish interrupted "I've seen four so far. Look there's five…All shared, All belong."

He muttered, as he continued intensely with the game, oblivious to anything Jasper may have seen.

Chapter Nine

The Council

Jasper's trembling finger pointed to the horizon and Jish saw the panic etched on his features and realised that Jasper was no longer playing.

Alarm welled up inside making Jish feel sick as Jasper shouted hysterically, "Look! A Devlin army with spears and feathers attached…Look! Hundreds!"

He grabbed his horizon viewer and looked through the two carefully crafted crystal lenses from Myreellien. He could just make out the short, stubby, leather-clad figures with their thick, wrinkled skin. They were about a halfpels' journey away on foot.

"It's just as well they've never learned to tame the zellifer the way the Ilves have," he shuddered to himself as Jish snatched the viewers from his cold, clammy hands.

Even if Jish had never seen the ancient illustrations in the Lore Book he would still have known, "Devlins!" he mouthed the menacing words silently, the look of horror on his face echoing that of Jasper's. Neither spoke, both seemed frozen in the ghastly moment forever.

"Quick!" Jasper finally leapt up. "We must tell Twit immediately."

"But he's with Princess Zithanduel for the Affirmation. D'you mind what happened the…" Jish started as he remembered a previous time they had interrupted the Affirmation.

"We'll be in even more trouble if we don't…We'll have to transfly." Jasper interrupted harshly. "Let's go"

Jish followed. He had learnt to listen to Jasper, over the many yer they had been companions, and knew it was pointless arguing or reasoning with him.

Still, as he followed, he shouted his objections anyway, "We'll get it fir this! Y'know we're not meant to without his permission." Jasper being twenty yer older and wiser than Jish knew that this was a minor consideration and an occasion when rules were meant to be broken.

Transflighting as never before they darted and dived around the branches of Quelwood and Limebrack trees in the Forest of Time, alongside the Lake of Life. When they reached Welhspring, they did not stop in the Upper Entrance Hall, as was customary, but flew on down through the maze of corridors and taking short cuts they knew would take them directly to the Chamber of the Great Welhspring Hall, where Princess Zithanduel conducted her daily administrations.

The Timewatcher looked up, eyes flashing with utter disbelief but as he was about to launch into a vicious tirade Zithanduel put up her hand and silenced him with a regal smile.

"Please, Jasper, speak! I know you must have a very important reason for your unexpected arrival," she said warmly.

Jasper flashed her a grateful smile and turned to face his stern master clearly stating the devastating explanation for the untimely interruption.

"The Devlins are coming, Sir! We have seen them on the horizon." He and Jish were performing a hurried elevation and bow but Jish bumbled breathlessly, an edge of rising panic in his shaky voice, "There are about a hundred of 'un with spears looking ready for battle as 'tis foretold! Highness."

The Princess smiled reassuringly at them and fixing the two frightened Keepers with her clear blue eyes, conveyed calmness although Jasper glimpsed something unfathomable he had never previously seen in her eyes. "Keepers, the Timewatcher has trained you well." She cast him a grateful, appreciative look, which made him blush, much to the amusement of Jasper and Jish.

She continued addressing them, ignoring his embarrassment, "You will need all the skills you have learned if you are to fulfil the Quest to eradicate the Devlins from this land forever. Your task will be exhausting and you will believe it is beyond you. But the Chosen Ones are here. Now is the expected time. You are more than capable."

She turned her attention away from the Keepers and facing the Timewatcher voiced a command, "Call a meeting of the Council of Elders in the Great Hall! Ensure that the Chosen Ones are present." With that, she turned and left.

Emeriel, Jes and Jenna were resting in the Glade of Gillilien, gazing out at the distant Tower, blissfully unaware of the unfolding events. Jes lay on a grassy delphimillium covered bank, the delicate, purple, trumpet-shaped flowers dancing in the breeze around him. He looked across the Fountain of the Orb and lazily admired the view wondering about the distant Tower's purpose. He kept rubbing his scar, which suddenly started to ache for some inexplicable reason.

A fountain of water propelled the Orb from below and Emeriel was questioning how such a heavy looking, crystal ball could be held up by such a fine jet of water. She watched the ball turning over and over without any sign of an upward or downward motion.

Jenna was making a chain of dairiels, carefully threading the tiny blue flowers through one another with great concentration, as the stems were so fine. The tall, yellow hail-wort flowers were bobbing around in the faint breeze.

Emeriel watched Jenna and then heard her silent thoughts, "I'll give this necklace to the pretty lady with the golden hair and then I'll make another for Emeriel. She looks so sad."

"I'm fine." Emeriel said, not entirely truthfully.

Jenna looked up with a start having forgotten Emeriel's Gifft in her moment of relaxation. "It's very annoying you know," she snapped irritably.

"I know. I'm sorry" Emeriel sympathised, "But I thought you might have forgotten and it seemed rude not to remind you. Anyway, I'm trying to find ways this might be useful and am still practising." She went on, excusing herself.

At that moment Methven appeared and Emeriel's face turned ashen as she leapt up, exclaiming, "The Devlins are here. Aren't they? Who are they?"

She demanded. "I can feel your fear, Methven."

Jes and Jenna were mystified at this reaction from Emeriel, although by now, they realised she must have interpreted his thoughts and deduced she was afraid of what she had learned. The scar on Jes arm was irritating again.

Methven sighed and sat down heavily on the bank. Emeriel considered he appeared older as she viewed him across the spray.

"We don't have much time but you deserve to know your involvement." He muttered quietly, as though to himself.

"The Devlins, or Dreaded Race, as they are known to those who fear to utter such an evil name, are descended from the Faerspring race, many hundreds of yer ago. They were banished by Justice in the Yer of the Bock Thorn. They were a small group of Faeries, led by Drevilarche, who misused his powers of transflight and thought reading. He tried to overcome the Wise One in the Temple of the Beloved Sisterhood, and attempted to poison the minds of the Elders in the Gathring, by planting false thoughts supposedly from the Wise One, in order to usurp his powers. He poisoned the children on Faerspring. Justice banished him, but Drevilarche took with him the Stone of Nelwife and since then no children have been born on Faerspring."

He looked saddened as he spoke and although he had put a thought block on, Emeriel could feel his pain and knew there was much he could not tell. Jes and Jenna were both looking thoughtful and Emeriel knew that Jenna was thinking about the children and where this place might be. Jes was wondering what Devlins were like and how powerful they were. He rubbed his arm absently.

Methven stood, saying, "Now, no delay, we must go!"

They glided behind him making a thoughtful, quiet, procession through the short glassy corridors to the Great Hall. Their amazing surroundings were of no consequence beside their contemplations of this new knowledge.

Green sunlight flooded the Great Hall, eerily lighting the faces of the gathered Elders. A large round table of marble now replaced the throne. Ten Elders were seated, wearing the most colourful, dazzling, gem-studded headbands and long, enveloping cloaks, thin and flowing, shimmering the deepest green they had ever seen, having a mysterious, metallic quality.

Emeriel heard Methven's thought directed toward her, "Armour. An indication of the seriousness with which the Council regard this!"

She thought, "It looks like cloth, not armour."

He replied, "Yes. Faerie armour."

Zithanduel drifted in and swiftly took her place as the High Chieftanna. She caught the Council off guard and they could not perform the ritual bow with sufficient speed. She seemed not to notice.

The carving on the smooth, shiny table distracted Jes. There was a view at each place setting, of woodland, coast or mountain. As he gazed, he realised there was movement in each carving, rivers flowing and wind blowing. Zithanduel's place carving was of Welhspring and extended into the centrepiece, in one continuous design. Words were written in the Ancient script;

Ζιτηανδυελ οφ Ωελησπρινγ

at the High Chieftanna's and others but, since he did not understand the script, Jes could only remember the inscription at her placing.

Zithanduel was already talking. Emeriel nudged Jes to make him concentrate. "Welcome, friends. I called this Council of the Elders of the Gathring to make our plans to assist the Chosen Ones but now I must, in addition, formally announce the arrival of the Dreaded Race on Faerspring once more. Some of you are already aware of this. We meet to discuss and formulate our response and defence."

A grey-haired, wizened Faerie spoke, voice trembling, "Highness, we need to invoke the Master Gifft Scholars and engage their help." He pointed toward a setting with an inscription that read;

Μαστερ Γιφφτ Σχηολαρσ.

Within the carving, Jes could see a group of Faeries in a purple swirling mist, wearing tall, pointed purple hats. They were pouring over a large old book, busily throwing odd objects including animal body parts into a cauldron.

Emeriel had noticed, too, and was amazed as well as frustrated, having realised by now that a thought block had been cast across the meeting of the Council, presumably so all could participate on an equal basis. Annoyingly though, it prevented her from asking Methven any of the burning questions.

"Yes. Glerendel and also the Chosen Ones." Zithanduel replied, causing Emeriel and Jes focus once more. Jenna was already completely absorbed with Zithanduel and had been from the moment the Chieftanna had arrived.

"I have invited the Chosen Ones to the Gathring so that we might ask for their help. Methven would you please seat them." She indicated three vacant places and Methven led Emeriel to a place setting illustrating a dark fortress on an Island and bearing the inscription;

Εμεριελ Χηοσεν Ονε .

Jes was led to a more familiar scene depicting the secret doorway in Grandma's garden. It made the hair on the nape of his neck stand on end. He read;

ϑεσ Χηοσεν Ονε.

Jenna was taken, still gazing agog at Princess Zithanduel, to a setting with a view of snowy covered Mountains, and inscribed;

ϑεννα Χηοσεν Ονε.

There was no time to reflect as the High Chieftanna continued, "To the point! We need your help Chosen Ones. From the Lore we know there are tasks to be undertaken in order to rid us of the dark powers of the Devlins, which only you are able to accomplish.

"We can, I believe, with the help of the Master Gifft Scholars, keep them at bay here for a time, but in order to achieve freedom from their evil grip we must ask much of you. Your mission will be dangerous and costly but there is no other way."

All eyes in the room were upon them, questioningly with a desperate, eager hope.

Chapter Ten

The Commitment

A bright, shimmering of kaleidoscopic colours preceded a brilliant white light. Ellie, Tom and Joanne found themselves looking at each other, in their former child-like state. The Council had disappeared, and encircled by a grey world of mist and cloud, they were looking down at the landmass of Faerspring with another Island to the Nilh. Tom was acutely aware that the wound on his arm had reopened and was trickling again, but kept this to himself as Methven appeared beside them.

Ellie stated, "We're being allowed to chose. Aren't we? As ourselves I mean."

Methven nodded, smiling at her intuition.

"We don't want you to feel pressured."

Without a moment's consideration, Tom said, "Let's do it. It'll be exciting!"

Ellie glowered at Tom, " You never consider the consequences to yourself or others, do you? Stop and think, for once. What about Jo and I? This is going to be dangerous. I'm not sure."

Jo looked at Ellie, "If we don't they will lose their lovely world. They've already lost their children."

"Yes," Tom joined in, feeling guilty for being so selfish, and wanting to redeem himself with Ellie, "Think about the children." He looked at Ellie, hoping for a more positive response. Jo, too, was silently pleading and Ellie knew they had to help, "If we are all sure?"

The three children, despite their fears, reached out to one another in the grip they used at home to indicate they had a pact and found themselves transfigured immediately to their places at the Gathring. Methven smiled gratefully.

Emeriel found herself saying confidently to Zithanduel, "Your Highness, we would be honoured to help. Please tell us what we may do." Relief swept around the table palpably confirming the three in their commitment.

Zithanduel spoke, softly, "We are grateful to you." The Elders nodded their agreement.

"First, you must get the Ancient Book of Lore and Flowers of Faerspring. You will need to visit Princess Rhianne on Faer Isle. Please take our Greetings to my sister. Ask her if she will read and translate the passages of the Lore relating to the destruction of the Dreaded Race. Only then will you know what is required of you. It may be that these passages are not yet revealed but she will be pleased to share what she can with you."

"Does no-one else understand this Ancient Book of… what was it?" queried Emeriel.

"The Ancient Book of Lore and Flowers of Faerspring" Zithanduel prompted, laughing. Such a beautiful tinkling sound, thought Jenna, still completely bemused by this delicate Faerie Queen.

"The Timewatcher is responsible for the Lore and knows all the manuscript but is unable to translate the Chapter relating to the Destruction of the Dreaded Race. It is written in an Ancient tongue. Only one on Faerspring knows this; Rhianne can help. Ariella is able to help with many of the earlier passages."

"Fine! Let's go!" said Jes rising impatiently. He was bored with all the ritualistic talk and was eager to tackle the task. His wound had miraculously healed again but his scar was irritating him once more and he wanted to be off.

Zithanduel indicated he should sit. Emeriel detected a slight edge of impatience in this and watched as Zithanduel turned towards a younger Elder, "Omendar," she began, as though Jes had never spoken. "Please would you explain the travel arrangements to our friends."

Omendar was short. He blushed as he stood. He was keen and bright, with crystal lenses, which had the effect of making his green Faerie eyes, seem huge, bug-like and intelligent. Now it was Emeriel's turn to be absorbed.

Omendar spoke, "It is not possible to travel the distances involved in your quest by transflight. It would take too long. Also, transflight is impossible in many of the terrains you must cross. The most energy efficient, time saving and life preserving way is by Lorduress."

He pointed towards Jenna's place setting, his words seemed to be illustrated as a dim, hazy creature was flapping it's way across the wooden scene. None of them could make out what it was exactly but Jenna was enthralled to see this creature and knew instantly it was of great importance to the success or failure of their mission.

Omendar continued with authority. (Emeriel could not help but be impressed by his confidence), "I will see that the Lorduress is saddled for the five of you..."

"Five!" Jes interjected.

"Yes," Zithanduel replied. "You will be accompanied by the Keepers who will protect the Lore Book. They have been well trained for their task and know what is expected of them. You will meet them shortly."

"Highness?" Another of the Elders was speaking, a gangly looking Faerie with skin much swarthier than the others. His ears were more pointed and limbs longer, Emeriel thought he looked more elf-like.

"Yes, Emanuain?" He had Zithanduel's full attention.

"Should they forewarn Ariella in Ilvwood? They may need Ilve help for the journey to Faer Isle, since it is such a dangerous route?"

Omendar turned towards Emanuain and said "You are right they must travel to Ilvwood, immediately!"

Zithanduel nodded her agreement, adding, "I think they should forewarn Elhspring as well. They should know in order to protect themselves. We may also need their aid in our plight."

Emanuain replied, "Yes and…"

But Zithanduel raised her right hand, silencing him and the other Elders who had begun to debate the issues amongst themselves. "These are important details but the Master Gifft Scholars must be summoned from Jezzithra immediately, we have no time to lose, the Devlins are advancing as we speak."

Emeriel couldn't help but notice that a number of Elders froze with fright and looked over their shoulders at the very mention of the dreaded Devlin advance.

Zithanduel continued, seeming not to notice. "It is imperative we find a way of prolonging or halting their march so that our friends can complete their mission in time. If we fail, all will be lost!"

Zithanduel produced a crystal box from a pocket within her fine gold robe and placed it in the centre of the setting with the inscription;

Μαστερ Γιφφτ Σχηολαρσ.

She stood and cast her arms in practiced movements around the glowing, glistening crystal box, and chanted, almost inaudibly,

"Μαστερ Γιφφτ Σχηολαρσ, χομε φορτη ωε ηαωε νεεδ οφ ψου."

She repeated the incantation, three times. At that, the air above the crystal box shifted and swirled, appearing to swallow up the scene of the Gifft Scholars into a whirl of mist, which spiralled upwards becoming denser and denser until a purple-hooded face began to form.

"We hear you High Chieftanna Zithanduel and await your command." Behind the hooded face, the other Master Gifft Scholars were gathered in their pointed hats.

"The Dreaded Race has arrived and is seen on the horizon from the Timewatcher's Tower, a halfpel's journey away. We ask you to find a way to delay them, so that the Chosen Ones who have now arrived may destroy them."

She indicated Emeriel, Jes and Jenna and the shadowy group came sweeping across the table to inspect them closely. This was extremely unnerving and Jenna almost burst into tears at seeing these wrinkly old faces so close to her own.

"We have decided they should journey to Ilvwood and then on to Faer Isle to where they will await instruction from the Lore." Her voice went quiet, almost to a hush as she continued. "Anything you can do to lessen the hazardous nature of their quest would be greatly appreciated."

"You ask much of them…and us, Your Highness." The hooded face, now much clearer, replied carefully. He had bushy grey eyebrows bristling above green eyes encased in deep wrinkles, which sparkled nevertheless. "We should be able to delay the Dreaded Race by creating an invisible fence around them."

He paused as though considering the difficulties and implications. "We can probably maintain that for five pel but it will take our combined forces to hold it and will leave our power much depleted. We will not be able to perform any other requests in the meantime."

A further thoughtful pause followed. "We will, in addition, permit Renewil the Owline to travel with the Chosen Ones and also the Jewel of Nilhspring, for their protection and guidance. Renewil knows well its qualities and abilities. There may be other invocations we could employ to hold the Dreaded Ones, Highness, but we would need time to devise and conjure them."

"I understand," she began, " Alas I fear, time is the one thing we lack. As ever, you have been most kind and helpful." The bushy eye-browed face broke into a gentle smile and Jenna no longer felt frightened. "When will you be able to perform these requests?"

"Immediately, Highness," he responded. "We see their location. We would ask you not to contact us again unless it is a matter of dire urgency, so that we may preserve our energies for the fence. Renewil will bring the Jewel to the Journeying Ones as they travel. We wish you speed, success and safety." He finished by addressing Emeriel, Jes and Jenna.

Then the Gifft Scholars bowed and receded into the swirling mists and the scene where they could be visualised, locked arm in arm in a circle, heads bowed, a thick blue mist enveloping them.

The Gathring turned to look at Emeriel, Jes and Jenna with a strange mixture of hope and concern in their eyes. There was silence in the Hall, for what seemed like an eternity, each considering what might lie ahead, but none feeling more apprehensive than the Chosen Ones.

Finally Zithanduel spoke firmly with authority, "No delay. Etheriel?" She engaged a wise-looking lady with sharp features, even for a Faerie, and short, sharp black hair, "Please, summon the Timewatcher and the Keepers. Omendar would you announce that I wish to speak to the Citizens forthwith?"

She waved her hand high in the air and was gone. Those remaining stood. The table vanished. Emeriel had barely time to flash a question to Methven, "What is Renewil?" But, before he could reply, the Great Welhspring Hall began to fill and it was only a matter of moments before all were assembled, Emeriel couldn't help thinking that thought speech must have been employed to communicate for the crowd to have gathered so quickly.

Once more Zithanduel descended regally from above and began swiftly, "My people, I thank you for attending. Many of you will have realised from the Summoning that the Devlins are coming." A united sharp intake of breath went up from the fearful crowd and Emeriel couldn't help thinking that many of them had obviously not realised.

"There is no cause for panic, the Chosen Ones are here. However we must prepare ourselves for the tasks ahead. The Chosen One's and the Keepers will be departing soon for Elhspring, whilst our Master Gifft Scholars halt the progress of these miserable creatures.

"Those of us here must set to work to mask Welhspring and conjure up our defence petitions. Those of you with protection Giffts must assemble around the perimeter. On your behalf, I would like to convey our good wishes and prayers for the safe return of those who are journeying for us.

"Everyone should know what he or she must do. To your places! You are all free to leave, except those who are journeying and Methven. We will have the celebration we proposed for tonel in their honour, on their return instead. May Justice be with us all."

The crowd dispersed quickly, looking sympathetically and gratefully at those remaining; an almost sad look in many eyes that was really disconcerting, even Jes was lacking bravado at this juncture. The last midpel had brought little to be glad about. In fact, the sense of foreboding and fear was overwhelming.

Eventually, only Methven and two unknown figures were remaining with Emeriel, Jes and Jenna. That was when the trouble started.

Chapter Eleven

The Departure

Emeriel and Jish took an instant and unexpected dislike to each other. Methven could see how it had happened, Emeriel, being inexperienced in thought speech and not yet having developed her latent Gifft of thought blocking, had struck the first blow, inadvertently. She had been studying the Keepers, as had Jes and Jenna, and each had made their own astute assessment and observation.

Emeriel had looked at Jish and thought, "What strange colour eyes? Deep purple, how odd? Can he be trusted?"

This was met with a "Well you don't look s'smart yersel!" and a glare from the dark velvety eyes, with their long dark lashes, was fired back across the intervening space.

Methven instantly felt the electric atmosphere and, having heard the interchange, knew there would be frequent stormy times ahead. Trying to make amends, he belatedly began introductions. Despite his efforts, Emeriel fired back a look that usually stunned Jenna into immediate submission and was not lost on Jish who continued to glower.

Emeriel slammed her first thought block on, although was unsure how she had managed it and Methven could not help reflecting it was a shame she had learnt it at this precise moment, since he had glimpsed regret before it had come into action. However, Jish was far too busy disliking her, to have noticed. Emeriel was thinking she should make an immediate apology, for such uncharitable thoughts and explain that she was only a novice with regard to thought speech. It was way too late for that unfortunately!

Methven did his utmost to rescue the situation, politely intervening, "Shall we go and sit in the garden within the Glade of Gillilien? I'll arrange that we eat together there and you can all get to know each other better."

Jes liked the way eating was the answer to most issues on Faerspring; he was really beginning to settle into their lifestyle. He was oblivious to the rumbling problems. Jenna was not, and she had seen the familiar glare Jish had been treated to and thought that Methven's suggestion was essential if they were ever going to get on together so she added her enthusiastic agreement along with Jes'.

"Good!" Methven said, relieved. "I'm sure you'll all get on splendidly."

"Not likely," thought Emeriel, fortunately with a thought block in place. She was learning fast, continuing the block as she assessed Jasper. He looked more open and amiable, with fine, blonde, curling hair, light blue-lilac eyes and, taller than Jish, he also looked tougher and stronger in a frail-faerie way, of course. She noticed that Jes and Jenna were instantly relaxed by his friendly grin.

They returned to the Garden, following Methven through a crystal archway entwined with scented, deep red climbing rosafers. Now there were cushions and a low table, arranged welcomingly on the grassy bank. Despite the peace and tranquillity, they were conscious of Methven being keen to press on. Having witnessed the enemy themselves, Jasper and Jish were especially cognizant of the time pressure.

Gerianne transfigured and produced Crillis and Emerene, which, they now realised, was exceptional, such things being reserved for emergencies or specific purposes. Crillis and Emerene were so precious and rare.

Methven beckoned to Gerianne and Emeriel knew that they had communicated by thought when a healthy supply of pale blue Thistleberries appeared as well. She smiled wryly, realising why!

Jasper turned to Methven and asked, "How much time do we have, Methven? When do we leave?"

"I'm sorry to say, immediately. It is a long while since I have seen you both and I would have enjoyed catching up on your progress. Twit has told me you've come on well." Jasper and Jish chortled with laughter, hearing Methven use their own nickname for him.

"Who is Twit?" Jes wanted to know.

Jish held out his hand, responding to Jes' query, "The Timewatcher" and blew gently across his fragile palm and a hologram of the austere Twit appeared. Emeriel was impressed at this and the whole group fell about hysterically, seeing this serious looking figure associated with such a silly sounding name.

Methven hurried them, "Now eat up. Gerianne has packed more for the journey. We leave as soon as you have eaten. The Lorduress is saddled, I believe."

"Are you coming too?" Emeriel enquired and was relieved to hear his response, "As far as I am able." His eyes glazed as he spoke.

"Methven, do they know about the Lorduress, Ilvwood and Faer Isle?" Jish challenged, with a hint of arrogance, Emeriel thought. Methven sensed her disquiet and said, "A little, but we must teach them as we travel. If you are to thwart the Dreaded Race you will need to share knowledge and Giffts amongst you."

As they ate the Crillis, they were all beginning to feel its enlivening effect, which was really just as well. Jes also noticed his scar had stopped itching so much. The talk of the Dreaded Race made them nervous, but with the Emerene, which followed, they felt more relaxed and happy. Also, Emeriel noticed she felt more capable and prepared somehow. She had not noticed that effect the last time she had tasted it.

Now satisfied, Methven had their full attention as Gerianne tidied around them, "The Master Gifft Scholars have delayed the Devlins in accordance with Zithanduel's command."

Gerianne nearly dropped the Emerene Decanter at the very mention of the evil word.

"We will leave for Ilvwood and forewarn Elhspring en-route. It will take many pel to reach Faer Isle, even on the Lorduress!"

The Departure was a quiet affair; the dutiful citizens were masking the citadel as instructed. At least, it would have been quiet were it not for the

Lorduress, a beast felt and heard long before it became visible. They were led up several wooden escalators, (still an irresistible attraction to Jes) and as they ascended he became aware of a low, rumbling, growling sound with an increasingly vibrating quality.

The higher they went the more aware they became of the stomping, shuddering character of the noise. The light was also getting dimmer.

Emeriel briefly caught Jish's unguarded thoughts, the reason being he was so distracted by his fear and apprehension. "I hate this critter. Fell 'arf it last time en'it don't sound any smaller this time."

Abruptly, he became aware of Emeriel's intrusion and resented it. He looked furiously at her, instantly imposing a stern block. He was particularly annoyed that she knew he was afraid of the Lorduress and Emeriel had learned another valuable lesson about thought speech that it is rude to intrude without a good and necessary reason.

She had noticed though that Jasper was gentler in his approach, a flicker of a frown, a gentle reprimanding smile and then the block. She liked him for that, Jish on the other hand….

Her thoughts were interrupted. "What is that?" The vibration grew into a thunderous thudding as they neared the glass platform.

"That is a Lorduress!" Jish was staring at her. "It is what we will be on for some pel." She knew he was trying to scare her and he was achieving his aim. They were now on the transparent platform upon which they had arrived only two pel before. It seemed like ages ago.

Jes found himself gazing, in awe, at the most amazing creature he had ever seen or dreamt about. It was waddling off the platform with enormous bone shaking steps and it disappeared over the edge as Emeriel and Jenna came up the last wooden elevator. Gracefully the pair slid off the last step onto the platform, Jish and Jasper brought up the rear. Jish looked like he was about to get onto the worst ten-looped roller coaster ever, thought Jes, resorting to his earth memory for inspiration.

Jish, anxiously scanned the platform for the Lorduress, and caught sight of its scaly, sea green tail whipping across the far end, transiently. Despite his brief glimpse, he remembered it well and the way it had sent him flying into the Lake of the Trifilly, the last time they had met. Jes turned to follow Jish' petrified gaze and found himself staring at huge jaws full of sharp teeth.

As the giant scaly beast closed its mouth, it's nostrils flared, sending a puff of smoke, which although, obviously gentle compared to its capability, was enough to surround the group in billowing clouds of confusion. Emeriel could just make out its spiny backbone and folded wings.

The creature's liquid amber eyes, with their extra lid and black as night, slit-like pupils entranced Jenna. To everyone's astonishment, as the smoke was clearing, she walked bravely up to the monstrous head and spoke gently in its ear which necessitated her standing on tiptoes, "Hallo, I'm Jenna. I'm very pleased to meet you!"

Methven seemed bemused, fleetingly, and then stepped over promptly, robes flapping behind. "Loro, my old friend. Please let me introduce you to Jenna, Emeriel and Jes." Indicating them in turn. "I know you are already acquainted with Jasper and… err.. Jish."

Loro flicked his tail threateningly near to Jish, so that he almost fell over, winking at Jenna simultaneously. Jenna patted him gently over his long nuzzle and smoke flared gently in appreciation. Emeriel sniggered at Jish, who was furious with her and, of course, with Loro. She stepped forward to join Jenna. Loro eyed them all closely, too closely, Jes thought as the large fluidous eye stared at him, blinking slowly and subsequently caught him on the hop with a disarming wink.

Jish was now hiding behind Jasper's black travelling cloak and Loro licked his lips mischievously and had a little taste of Jish' leggings, humorously. This sent the entire group, including Methven who was making valiant efforts to avoid it, into side-splitting hilarity, except Jish, naturally, who was quite unable to appreciate the joke and was clinging to Jasper for dear life, a quivering wreck.

Emeriel was still tittering when Methven, finally regained his composure with considerable difficulty and spoke sternly to Loro,

"Ενουγη!

Loro's flapping wings and swishing tail calmed, becoming motionless. He floated to align himself gently alongside the platform. Between his shoulder blades, there was a saddle, if you could call it that, with a large, solid, leathery pad covered with cushions and drapes of deepest red. Methven indicated they should embark, and one by one, with great care they stepped out onto the hide step and clambered aboard.

Jes was first, his adventurous enthusiasm evident, followed by Jenna who had fallen in love with this fantastic creature. Jasper went next, feeling privileged to meet Loro anew.

Emeriel preceded the petrified Jish who was doing his utmost to conceal his terror and she could not resist a backward glance of disdain as she stepped onto the magnificent beast with confidence, and an essential thought block. She was really thinking, "I must be crazy!"

Methven, more or less, lifted the annoyed and distracted Jish up with him, before he had opportunity to change his mind. Jenna, meanwhile, had moved up to be immediately behind Loro's pointed ears and, from this vantage point, could see his amber eye moving around in amiable acknowledgement of her choice.

They were all trying to position themselves as comfortably and safely on the cushions as they could when Zithanduel made an unexpected appearance.

"Justice, speed you on your way!" She called, competing with the increasing noise of Loro unfurling his wings, which he started flapping excitedly.

Jenna whispered in Loro's ear, "Steady, Loro, poor Jish! He's terrified of you." He winked in reply and Jenna knew, of all the animals she had ever known and loved, he was one she would never forget. Despite her warning though, the poor unfortunate Jish was still trying to find the best possible position and was barely seated at this point. He would have been lost forever if Methven had not grabbed the cord around his waist, which resulted in him dangling perilously over the side of Loro's saddle. Emeriel screamed as Jasper caught hold of a piece of his blue leggings and helped Methven to haul Jish back on board. Loro turned his head languorously to give Jish a wicked, cheeky grin, breathing smoke, engulfing them all as he took off, climbing steeply.

They turned to wave to Zithanduel, silently realising that Welhspring was disappearing rapidly in the mist.

The Chosen Ones, especially, had an acute fear of the unknown; each was now wrapped in their own thoughts and worries. Methven and Jasper were sensitive to this. Jish was otherwise preoccupied. The rocking, rolling motion of a Lorduress' flight, coupled with the vertical movements from the powerful, muscular wings and an alternating swishing head and tail motion, usually had two effects, either extreme nausea or drowsiness.

After an exhausting quartpel, Jish felt extremely ill and the others, with the notable exception of Jenna, were soundly asleep. Jenna hugged as much of Loro's neck as she could, whispering in his ear and discovered that he could project his thoughts into her own. She learned of the Dragon Lore and how it related to the Dark Ones, "Devlins you mean."

He nodded, glancing fearfully over his shoulder and she heard his, "Never speak their name or they may see us." He explained that as well as the evil the Dark Ones had visited on Faerspring, they had also destroyed most of Loro's kind, and only a few now remained. His father, Loradurther, was the Lord of Ruthragon and he had sent Loro to defend Faerspring. He was very homesick, though, missing his family and the lush, verdant valleys and volcanoes on his homeland far, far away. He understood that she, too, was homesick and missed her Grandma and family. Their rapport increased with the passing pel.

Jish continued to feel Loro-sick and heaved over the side with uncomfortable regularity. Jenna divided her time between Loro and Jish, trying to comfort and console him, just the way her Grandma would have done back at home.

Eventually, at nelfall, the green glow, from one sun, and a bright yellow, from the other, settled on the horizon, with magnificent rainbow shades, the three had never witnessed before. Neither did they see them now, being fast asleep. Loro, although tired and thirsty, flew on unquestioningly, tirelessly, carrying his precious crew as the beautiful azure and bronze moons made their appearance in the nelsky. Throughout his long life, he had been trained by his father for this duty and he undertook it proudly. As he flew, he dreamed of home and the belching fiery volcanoes and brilliant ruby glow from the setting suns on his side of the globe. He focused on his destination on the coast, little by little, becoming visible to his ancient, far-seeing eyes.

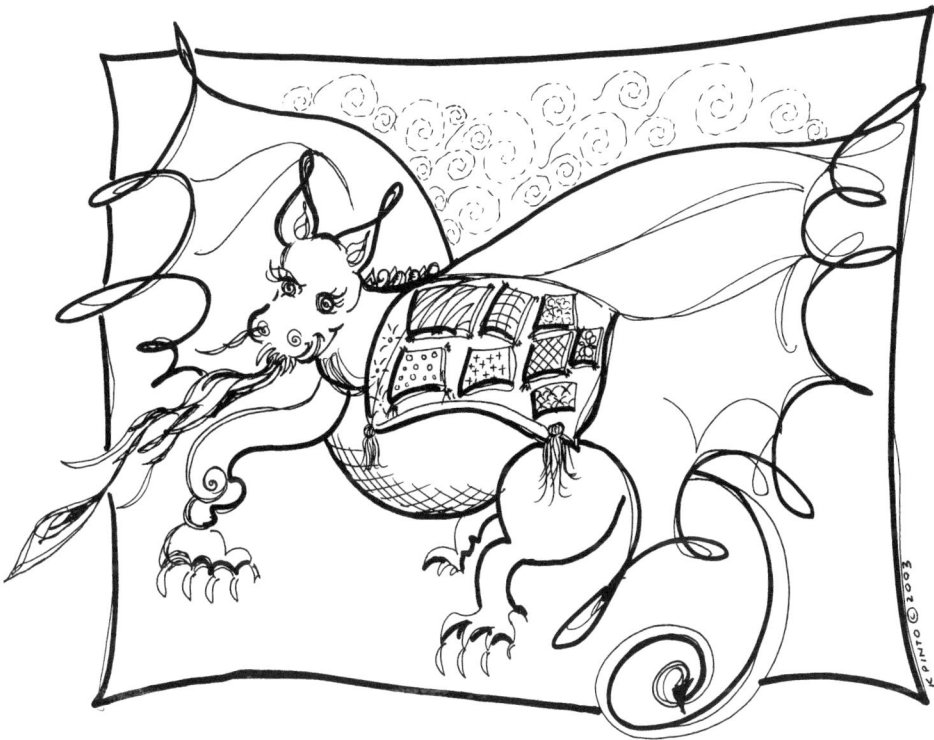

Chapter Twelve

Elhspring

By the time the bright yellow sun rose first in the Welh Loro was exhausted. One by one the sleepy group awoke. As soon as Jish aroused he promptly heaved again although there was nothing except a bilious fluid to vomit now. Dark circles were developing around his dull weary eyes. Jasper and Methven were trying to console him. Typically, Jes was still fast asleep, 'not a morning person' Grandma often commented. Emeriel had little sympathy for Jish' weakness and focused on the amazing views ahead so she was the first to notice Elhspring in the distant spectacular lime sunrise. There were multiple, stone towers of varying heights with clay-tiled three and four storey buildings between. It was easily visible from a distance because the town perched on the highest hill set amongst numerous hillsides and valleys. The others had become aware of her silent interest; even Jish had forgotten how ill he was feeling.

Methven nodded at Emeriel's question, "Elhspring! Town of my birth!" he said, proudly.

As they neared the beautiful town, its steep, precarious position became more apparent and its small, square shuttered windows could be seen. Loro seemed confident and familiar with his route. Deftly, weaving, between the rocky outcrops, initially, and then through the narrow streets between the towers, he carried them safely into Elhspring. He slowed, gliding gently considering his size, alighting on the top of the second highest tower. The first soared above them. He landed as delicately as a butterfly although an almighty thud rather gave it all away. Methven laughed, clearly pleased to be in his ancient hometown. Jish was first off, naturally, and he slid hurriedly down the shimmering, green scales landing in a relieved heap.

Loro looked down his long snout, nostrils flaring and smoking, with a kindly smile at Jish and nuzzled him. Jish was entirely unappreciative but the gesture was not lost on Jenna who rewarded him with a hug after sliding down his foreleg as though she'd disembarked from a Lorduress daily from birth, she whispered to him, "You must be tired and hungry. I'll get you some food and water."

The landing of a Lorduress had not gone unnoticed by the inhabitants of Elhspring. It was unusual to say the least and caused a great commotion in the narrow alleys and streets below. The last time he had been seen was at the Great Celebration of the Marriage of Ariella to Gerelf, the Ilfhead of Ilvwood many yer ago. Loro had been honoured to be the Bridal Carriage and recalled it well, and it was clear, looking at the cheering crowd below, that they did too!

Two hundred and seventy yer had passed since, but as Ruthven transfigured immediately adjacent to him, it seemed like only yesterpel. "Loro, you old rascal, how are you? You don't look a day older!" cried the delighted, wizened, old character, giving the Lorduress a hearty slap on the scales.

Loro was so thrilled to see him he gave an excited leap, wobbling precariously. This resulted in his remaining, forgotten passengers slipping off his long scaly spine landing helplessly at Ruthven's feet. Even Jish could see the funny side of this, especially as Emeriel looked embarrassed and disconcerted. Ruthven creased with laughter and chuckled. He was an excellent host, who could see the comic side of everything, which had been fortunate over the many sad yer he had witnessed. He picked them up, one by one.

"We have been expecting your arrival, though not quite like this. I'm Ruthven." He introduced himself to Emeriel, Jes and Jenna with a low formal bow. "Renewil has told me of your mission." And at that their seventh companion flapped into view, adding to the confusion and excitement. Loro was still lumbering around Ruthven enthusiastically to Jish' exasperation, for there was no safe haven for him without Loro static in one place.

Renewil careered clumsily into the party; neither precision flying nor accuracy was amongst his talents, as they would later come to recognise. At the same instant, a spinning black crystal floated into the midst of the distracted group. Dancing elegantly around them with mesmerising colours never seen in their earth rainbows, it was accompanied by explosions of intense brightness like fireworks.

Hurried glances at one another confirmed its presence was a mystery; each breath was held expectantly, Methven and Ruthven both looked worried. It disappeared as suddenly as it had arrived and equally unexpectedly. Subsequently, when they recalled their adventure together, this was the episode that caused the most arguments, as they simply could not agree on the order of events.

Before anyone could comment, the confusion magnified when another of Loro's old acquaintances, Torro, appeared. He was a miniature version of Loro. His back being at about Jes' knee height he accidentally engineered a collapse of Jes' legs with his mad dashing and weaving in and out of Loro's large clawed feet. He was completely unaware of Jes who was attempting to stand. He knocked him over again, whilst upending the others with his spiky tail.

They later reflected that it was the ideal moment for the crystal to reappear. Bobbing around again, it emitted dazzling flashes of light, which were of increasingly dark colours until only an inky black shower of flames and belching smoke could be seen, like silhouettes.

Methven had leapt protectively to the front of the group, he looked to be too old to be capable of such agility, but he drew a green globe from his cloak and threw it at the darting crystal. For a while the crystal and globe seemed locked, as they darted and dived, the globe attempting to keep alongside the ever-darkening crystal but then there was a combat of sorts, showers of light and dark and sooty black smoke swallowed up the globe. Then they were all engulfed in darkness and silence. Somehow each of them was engaged in their own personal mind battle with the crystal.

Jes battled with intense fear and was paralysed; a feeling like ice seemed to sweep over him, from his feet upwards, along with a deep sense of foreboding. Then he was locked into a battle with a hoard of bats. His wound was flowing profusely and he sensed he was losing consciousness as he bled.

Jenna attempted to escape from the darkness and could see Loro under attack from a swarm of buzzing insects, trying to get under his scales, torturing him. She was screaming but not heard, she was trying to reach out to help him but could not move.

Jasper tried to find his way through the darkness and found himself in the Timewatchers' Tower surrounded by the Dreaded Ones who were trying to steal the Lilly. He was locked in a bloody fight with twenty of them, using a decorative sword from the wall of the Tower Hall. It was useless, not sharp enough to cut through their thick hides.

Jish, meanwhile, was back on Loro's back but horrifyingly was flying alone through the Forest of the Black Gobylins, with trees and their branches clawing at his back and poor Loro weaving his way valiantly through. Jish was feeling so sick but knew that if he let go he would fall into the hungry Venlintrap trees.

Methven was locked in a vicious but real contretemps with the crystal, which was attempting to create a transfiguration tunnel around Emeriel, Jes and Jenna. The crystal was sending fiery darts at him as he tried to stop it. He was being burnt and scarred by its intense heat but would not surrender. He was desperately trying to incant and lock the crystal in position but there was dark evil here, which he knew meant the Devlins were back in tow with the Prince of Death again. It was useless, but he would fight to the last breath.

He turned toward a glimmer of light and held out his wiry arm to try and absorb it and cast it at the inky crystal. It used all his energy and pained his mind and soul, as there was so little light and trying to concentrate it and use it, as a weapon was an almost impossible feat. He succeeded against the odds momentarily, and the tunnel was disrupted. The crystal went into frenzy and more pitch-black smoke erupted from it engulfing the group and the shaft of light. Methven could see that only Emeriel remained partially within the Transfiguration Tunnel but the crystal was weaving furiously again and she was becoming engulfed.

Emeriel, like Methven, whilst engulfed in the crystal's dark smoke, could see the reality of what was happening. She knew Methven was trying to save them and she watched the battle taking place between him and the power of the crystal. She saw the final moments, too. Methven fell and landed on a rocky outcrop, below the stone tower. He was engaged in a fierce fight with a black-cloaked force, wielding a spear, fire flaming at its tip. She watched helplessly, as he was further scorched.

She heard his silent thoughts in her terrified mind, "You will never overcome us, even with the help of these stupid Devlins. They don't know any better!"

She heard the dark force reply, "You will die, Methven! You and all your kind."

A pain seared through her brain as she heard the thought. It overwhelmed her and she passed into unconsciousness.

She blinked and became aware of a window with blank iron bars across it. There was a damp stench of old fish and decaying flesh. She turned her head and saw a heavy, wooden door. There was a small stool. The crystal still spun about her, close to her face. She hit it away, determinedly.

A face appeared in the darkness of the crystal and glowered threateningly back at her. She knew it was a power more evil than anything she had ever encountered. It was crowned with a black-gemmed spiked crown but the face although indistinct was threateningly fearsome.

At that same moment, the cloud of darkness swamping the friends at Elhspring lifted briefly and the dazed group became aware that Methven and Emeriel had disappeared.

The crystal returned spinning in an even more agitated fashion around Jes and Jenna. Jes was terrified, Emeriel was gone, and he was not about to lose Jenna, too. The return of the thick smoke catapulted him into action. He fixed his eyes on the crystal and used his raw and untrained Gifft of transobjection to shift the crystal. Initially, it was barely perceptible but he focused again, deep gloom almost overwhelming him and held the crystal still, preventing it from weaving around them both and then he felt a power come upon him, enabling him to hurl the crystal mentally at the tallest tower. It shattered into a million pieces; each emitting black plumes of smoke.

The remaining group were shocked and stunned. Despite their private agony, they had all witnessed the battle involving Methven and the dark power and knew that a previously unknown evil had visited them.

Ruthven spoke, into the dazed silence, "Follow me! Quickly! The Master Gifft Scholars told of this. We are not safe here. Please follow me!" He sounded desperate.

They had little choice but to follow him through an archway, in the stone tower, as he shouted to Loro, " We will need you later. I will send for you my friend." At that Loro took off sadly, shaking his head and sympathetically winked at the sorry crew as he flew overhead. He swept down into one of the valleys radiating from the hill town and was lost from view and their thoughts, as they concentrated on pursuing Ruthven, down the winding stone steps, before they lost him.

Down and down they went, glimpsing other buildings through slit-like windows made of thickened circular glass, like bottle ends, Jenna mused distractedly. Glancing at Jes' disappearing back she refocused and held tightly onto the rail on the wall to prevent Torro from tripping her up. Renewil was in great difficulty, clumsily careering into the wall at virtually every turn with an agonised screech.

The group poured out of the stair well onto the ground in a muddled huddle as Ruthven stopped abruptly in front of them. They were in a rectangular hall with a stone flagged floor. As they unravelled their tangled limbs from the inelegant heap, Jasper noticed the refectory table, heavy wooden chairs and the huge stone fireplace with a grate, full of enormous logs sparking away merrily. It was an inviting cheery welcome and a stark contrast to their downcast mood.

"Where's Emeriel?" Jenna sobbed, directing her question to Ruthven's strangely familiar face. It was already obvious that he was Methven's brother, even to Jes who was usually unobservant; they were so alike in appearance and mannerisms. It was an assumption on her part, albeit a correct one, and the others had noticed too. She did not care about any of that now though, only that her beloved Emeriel had vanished.

"I do not know Jenna. But Methven is also gone and I suspect and sense he is lost forever!" Ruthven was shaking his head in despair and Jenna felt guilty she had spoken without any consideration for his feelings. He continued, "We will find Emeriel I am sure, but we will need Ariella's help. Do you have the Lore Book, Jasper? We will need her to interpret it for us. The chapters, pertaining to the Devlin's arrival and Emeriel's disappearance, need translation by someone Giffted in the Ancient Lore. Ariella, as the High Chieftanna's sister, will help."

Jenna was furious, "Yo...Y...You mean you knew this would happen to Emer..Ellie and you just let it happen?"

Ruthven turned and laid a comforting arm on her shoulder, "Jenna much more is to come. You are needed to help us right a wrong, committed by the Dreaded Race. Emeriel is caught up in their wicked plans. We knew it would not be an easy path for the Chosen Ones, but not precisely what would happen. That is why we could not prevent it, which is why it is imperative you reach Ariella by nelfall. I will show you a secret tunnel."

His voice lowered to a barely audible whisper as he turned to include the whole bewildered group. "It is deadly and dangerous, now they know where you are." They were horrified at their losses and still in shock.

Jes wondered why he had ever gone into the hidey-hole at the end of the garden. It was his fault. Ellie had warned him and now she was gone. Why hadn't he listened? How were they going to manage now?

"Ruthven will you come with us?" The rest of the group pleaded and begged in unison, as the prospect of going on alone tore at them.

Ruthven shook his head firmly, "I must stay and protect Elhspring. Zithanduel will need me, now that Methven is gone." Tears welled up in his desolate eyes, as he spoke but he hastily brushed them away with the back of his hand, hoping they had not noticed. Despite their overwhelming fear, seeing Ruthven's bravery spurred them on and there was a steadfast determination about the group now.

Jasper and Jish knew they were about to face their life's challenge and that they would need all their training and hard-learned knowledge. Jes and Jenna were frightened but had no option but to continue on if they were to bring Emeriel back.

They followed Ruthven's disappearing figure without further debate, through the archway in the wall, which appeared from nowhere as he pressed an ornate carving over the fireplace. It was a low arch but only Ruthven and Jasper had to stoop to pass through. It was dark and musty inside the passageway. Cobwebs brushed softly against their arms and legs. Jenna crept close behind Jes, for protection. The mad Torro followed, with Renewil bringing up the rear crashing blindly into the walls at every turn.

"You OK?" Jes turned to Jenna.

"No! I'm worried about Emeriel and I hate the dark!"

"Don't forget how tough she is, even as Ellie she is a tough cookie. I think the Devlins will wish they had captured someone else. We'll get her back," He sounded confident though really he was sick to his stomach, wondering if she, too, was gone forever.

Chapter Thirteen

Fortress of Goth Devlin

Meanwhile, Emeriel was not feeling like a tough cookie, or indeed anything else remotely tough. Dirty, smudged tears streaked her face. She was lost, lonely, scared and hungry; hidden in a dungeon cell in the Fortress of Goth Devlin.

She had watched Methven fight for her life and, in the process, lose his own. She had taken off her garland and was suddenly feeling like Ellie again, she could not fathom out how she came to be in this awful place. Fresh tears flooded in grubby rivers down her face as she wept inconsolably. But after a while the sobbing subsided. Her natural strength and optimism sparked faintly and a glimmer of hope returned. She lifted her defiant chin and started to search around the barred cell for an escape route.

She could hear disturbing, thudding, metallic sounds far below; a deep, dark, shuddering filled her soul. Engine-like, it was repetitive, thundering, swamping her with a sense of foreboding. This was not as great as the immediate unease caused by the nearby, scratching noises. They were much more terrifying, mouse-like, and whilst Jenna loved mice and rats, Emeriel did not!! As she listened to the scurrying in the dark, unseen corners, she became aware of heavy, padding footsteps getting closer and more distinct until she knew with certainty that they were on the other side of the door.

Her mouth was dry, her heart paused, her breathing stopped as keys jingled and clinked clumsily in the large, metal lock. She watched intently as the key turned with a thunderous clunk. She gasped with fright as a grotesque, menacing creature stomped in, throwing the door forcefully back. It hit the stone wall, with an almighty crash. Emeriel shrank into the corner that had so horrified her moments earlier, hoping to hide. Furrowed, bony-browed eyes glared fiercely into hers. Fear almost overtook her. He towered above her and was twice her width. He moved slowly and clumsily, but that was of little consolation. He carried a fearsome assortment of devilish weaponry about him. His much-scarred, bare limbs were thick, stubby and wrinkly. He wore a black shiny tunic and an overtight, studded belt with a collection of knives attached but in his huge hand he held an awesome sword. To her great surprise, she realised that she knew what he was thinking and hastily put a thought block in place, in case he was Giffted too, though he did not look it!

"Not fair. Was my pellun. Was Dimmed's shift, not mine. Should be getting my wild boar sausage and thinpots now." As he looked at her, "She's nothing. Look at her! Wretch! He said she needed a close watch. He's mad as usual. Hate Faerspringuns."

Hearing this boosted Emeriel's failing courage for a short time. She kept tuned in to his thoughts and looked suitably frightened, hoping to learn as much as she could from him. He put a metal bowl of bread and water down, grunting grossly at her.

As he turned and left she heard his thought, "Now, where's the key? Is it on my belt or in the pocket?" She heard him fumble to lock the door, with difficulty and effort, "Aaah, there you go. Safely back on the hook, by the door, for next time. That'll keep Bigeviledd happy."

The thudding continued uninterrupted in the background and then intense scurrying broke out, as her cellmates realised food had arrived. Terrorised though she was, Emeriel snatched up the bowl before they could reach it. Shivering in the corner, she looked up at the grills on the high window, helplessly. The enormity of the situation hit her and she sobbed and sobbed impotently.

Eventually, out of hunger, she knew she must eat the bread and gulping on the dry, rancid morsels, she tried to piece together the events of the past few pel. She had been captured by the Devlins and now knew what they looked like, assuming her jailer was one. The face in the crystal that had battled with Methven was different but there was no doubting they were on the same side. If the jailer was typical of a Devlin, Emeriel had learned that, despite his size and girth, he was not bright and was preoccupied with food.

Her thoughts turned to where she might be, come to that where was Faerspring? Her mind wandered, until she fell into an exhausted, deep sleep.

She awoke feeling stiff, cold and very hungry. She realised, or thought she did, that not much time could have passed as it was still dark and there was no light shining through the window.

She did not know that the window opened onto a dark subterranean courtyard, surrounded by three storey buildings, built into the rock with only a few flickering torches to light it and a metal brazier in the centre. There were a few, cold Devlins huddled around this for warmth, one of them was Dedded, her jailer. Her cell was on the uppermost floor and had she known of their presence she still would not have been able to employ her Gifft or listen at such a distance.

Their conversation, if you could call it such, since they were not renowned as a race for their conversational skills or intelligence, revolved around whose turn it was to fetch more coal for the old brazier as the fire waned and whose turn it would be to take Emeriel's next meal. They tended toward laziness, probably, in part, due to their bulk, and the equal distribution of tasks, often occupied more time than the tasks themselves. An argument was breaking out then between Dedded, Dulledd and Brendded.

Their limited speech, coupled with their poor negotiating ability, meant that discussions of this nature generally had a fierce physical resolution and it was not long before they locked in the middle of a vicious knife fight, although being so thick skinned their wounds were insignificant and caused little deep injury. The daggers were carried to inflict damage on less well-protected adversaries like wild boar, zellifer or Faerspringians. In the end, the dispute was settled with the arrival of Sergeant Bigeviledd who exerted his authority over them, roaring loudly and abusively at them.

This was good news for the oblivious Emeriel, as it would mean the arrival of pelfirst, shortly. The bad news, though, was that Lord Madded had sent the command through the ranks to the Sergeant that he wished to interrogate the prisoner.

Brendded was sent to carry Emeriel's bread and water. Though taller and broader, he was as ugly as the other one, if that were possible. She again watched closely to learn whatever she could and it was as he turned to close the door she saw the extra eye at the back of his head behind his left ear. Apart from a tuft of spiky thick hair on top and thick curly bristles protruding from his disgusting nostrils, he was hairless.

"Eat and then come with me!" He grumped at her, turning back toward her. Emeriel saw an enormous mouth full of fangs and couldn't help thinking maybe that was why they mostly grunted inaudibly rather than spoke. She began to take confidence from the fact that despite their fearful appearance they may not be impossible to overcome given such limited abilities.

She employed her thought reading Gifft, managing to deduce his unhappiness with Dedded for making him come up so many stairs when it was not his turn; he was particularly difficult though and she could decipher nothing else, other than a series of grunting, growling, disjointed thoughts.

"Why?" She tried to engage him in conversation.

"Lord Madded said so!" he replied, blankly repeating Sergeant Bigeviledd's instructions.

He waited, impatiently, whilst she finished her pelfirst. Her hand brushed against her discarded garland and she surreptitiously slipped it on as he pushed her, roughly, towards the door. Her newfound confidence rapidly evaporated as she realised how dark it was and how futile an escape attempt would be. He had a dagger pressed firmly into her back and she had no idea where she was.

She decided to concentrate on possibilities for a future flight from this awful place. The stench of damp, excrement and rotting flesh was overwhelming as she entered the dark, dim corridor and combined to create a noxious effluvium that made her want to wretch. She was reminded of Jish and felt guilty for her unkind treatment toward him. He must have been feeling so ill. Too late for that now.

Brendded pushed her roughly, as she had paused briefly, onward through the long, dark corridor, a row of wooden doors on either side. There were lighted torches at every fifth door, insufficient to shed much light along the corridor.

To the left of each door was a large key. As she passed each cell she could hear the occupants, grunting noises from some and more intelligent thoughts of escape from others. Nearing the dark, dank corridor end, she noticed a gruesome splash of blood by the door and then to her alarm she heard a direct thought from the right.

"Are you Emeriel?"

"Yes. Who are you?"

"My name is Anuthel." In spite of being roughly shoved quickly past and on through a door she managed to catch, "Be very careful! Tell Lord Madded nothing."

Goth Devlin was a Fortress of stone, built on an inaccessible, formidable promontory in the Mountains of Dread on the Island of Goth Malin. Although it was mentioned in the Book of the Lore, few knew whether it really existed other than in legend. Treacherous waters on three sides surrounded the Fortress. The prison was set deep underground whilst Lord Madded's quarters were situated atop a square stone tower with a threatening jagged rampart, uppermost in the Fortress. Emeriel was forced through many poorly lit, winding tunnels which seemed to twist and turn in multiple directions but always ascending, such that despite her best efforts, she had no idea where she was.

She knew only that she must have been climbing somewhere very high. Finally, Brendded operated a lever hidden in the rock face, which opened a stone door. They went through and Emeriel was shocked to discover herself on a narrow precipice threading its way around a high-sided fort with an imposing tower. She looked and gasped seeing violent, crashing waves dashing at the black, vertical cliffs below. No means of escape there. She was right, for many souls had met their deaths trying to flee that way, none had ever left Goth Malin by sea alive. Gulls and eagles were spinning angrily overhead, battling against stormy winds above the towering walls of the Fortress. She noted there were no footholds in the walls.

There were intermittent claps of thunder and flashes of lightening. Another shove from Brendded reminded her of the narrow rocky path ahead, she concentrated hard, realising that if she lost her footing she would perish on the rocks beneath.

They wound their way around three sides of the fortress, before reaching a huge entrance with black metal doors and a large bolt across them. Twenty Devlins, standing on top of each other, could go through with ease. She had little time to consider this though as Brendded was knocking on a Devlin sized door using the hilt of his dagger.

As it opened, he pushed her anew into a gloomy courtyard, the crenellated tower rising threateningly above. It seemed that the thunder and lightening intensified at this point and a rainbow of black and grey tints appeared high in the dark stormy sky. The Devlin locked the smaller door behind them. She concluded that the fortress walls must be at least a room's width deep as she observed the rows of windows in the walls, which faced into the courtyard.

There was a red fiery haze tingeing everything, originating from the Tower walls, a pulsating glow permeating the surroundings. She had paused again, Brendded responded by thrusting her forcibly toward a door in the base of the Tower. It opened spontaneously, creaking loudly. Brendded drove her through it, slamming it shut behind them. She blinked in the darkness and found herself gazing into the evil black eyes she had seen in the Great Welhspring Hall place settings.

The face was bodiless, floating before her, red light shining from it. The face was similar to the other Devlins, except with larger, sharper fangs. She realised this was only a projected image but sensed that the head and body were nearby. She discovered that she could read this monster's thoughts, also. By their nature, they were dark thoughts and caused a pain in her head as she tried to discern them. She had difficulty determining anything clearly.

The Devlin intruded speaking in a thick, guttural voice.

"I am Lord Madded. You will tell me where the Lore Book is!"

"I'm Ellie and I'd like to go home to my grandma's, please." She bluffed politely, knowing perfectly well that she was Emeriel here. She would not tell him where the Lore Book was, even if she had known. She was suddenly appreciative of having the garland on and began to understand that in a strange way, it increased her courage and clarified her sense of identity.

She stuck with the Ellie routine and added a few tears for good effect. Lord Madded with all his apparent power seemed quite unable to disable this charade. He became increasingly angry and frustrated at being thwarted by this pathetic Faerspringian. He repeated his demand for the Lore Book and lost control of his temper bellowing loudly, under the ferocity of his attack she began to weaken.

However, Emeriel was determined to remain resolute, although it was getting harder to maintain the thought block. She continued to read his growing fury. The increased volume of his voice magnified the overall effect and the increased anger further exposed his fangs as he yelled.

He transfigured into his full personage and her fear escalated, courage waning. She stared at his incongruous, flowing, soft, black, leather cloak covering him head to foot and making him seem even larger. This though was preferable to looking at his face. Terror surged through her in sickening waves and she began to feel strange.

Her right foot tingled; she glanced down and discovered it had become invisible. She tried not to panic and as she calmed herself it reappeared. Unaware of this, Madded was incensed by her apparent lack of fear and roared at her until she had never felt more petrified in all her life. Now, both feet felt strange. She glanced down again. They had both disappeared. This time he noticed and towered above her in sheer fury as he realised that this Chosen One was Giffted in body cloaking.

Emeriel, now learning at speed how to body cloak, couldn't help thinking it might have been useful if Methven had taught her before, rather than discovering it like this! She allowed the panic to engulf her and, although it was draining and unpleasant, she disappeared from Lord Madded's view, leaving him behind in a rage that stormed tempestuously.

Brendded, who had been patiently waiting outside, was not to know what had occurred and thought he had better take a quick look to see what the roaring was about, besides he loved a good torture. He tried to defend his respected but dreaded Master when he could, already sporting several scars from his previous thoughtlessness in exactly such situations. He had learned nothing and was determined to help if possible this time. However, it seemed he had got it wrong yet again, the moment he opened the door Lord Madded went ballistic at him, throwing any object within reach with unfailing accuracy.

Emeriel seized her chance and moving silently, body cloaked, through the door, being careful to maintain her thought block. She looked around the courtyard for possible exits, but there was only the one way in and out. She wondered, as she ran across to the huge door, whether body cloaking allowed for passage through walls and the like. She tried it and found to her cost it did not! Fortunately, the bungling Brendded came to her rescue again.

The instant he had popped his head around the door and the familiar bellowing started he knew, despite his stupidity, what was coming. He stood for a few moments as his memory cell engaged slowly. This was when Emeriel seized her opportunity. Brendded then clumsily reversed his direction with what was a lightening reflex action for a Devlin, and beetled across the courtyard toward the only exit.

He fumbled with the key, unlocked the door and leaning on the heavy bolt, slid it across. Lord Madded was now back in crystal-like form and pursuing him, crossed the courtyard, but, before he could stop Brendded, the door was open and Emeriel stepped through, followed by Brendded, and the buzzing black crystal behind. Emeriel remained on the ledge, while Brendded retreated from his fuming master.

of diminutive figures with pointed ears and handcrafted, leaf hats and cloaks. The Ilves of Ilvwood, Jes realised with a start. He had not imagined they would look like this.

In their midst stood a taller lady, quite the most beautiful he had ever seen. Jasper too was smitten. She was like Zithanduel but younger with even finer features. Her long fair, flowing hair curled and reached her slender waist. She wore a pale green filmy dress, created from delicate, tiny leaves stitched painstakingly together, gathered by a fine gold cord at the waist; it shimmered and swept the ground as she moved. She wore a circlet around her hair with amber leaves matching exactly a design embroidered on her dress hem. Her arms were outstretched toward them in a gesture of welcome.

"We meet at last," she greeted them. "I have been expecting you for Faercenturies and here you are!"

"Sorry, we're late," said Jes, his cheekiness resurfacing, despite the obvious formality of the occasion. Jenna gave him the kind of look Emeriel would have supported proudly. Jasper knew that Ariella meant the Lore Book had foretold of this meeting and was so in awe after all he had read of her, that he slumped to his knees and bowed his head with reverence. Ariella embraced Jenna and smiled into her eyes, there was a familiarity to the look, and Jenna reminded herself that she was Zithanduel's sister.

"I am sorry about Emeriel, but even as we speak she is safe." The group were heartened. But although it was comforting, Jenna still wondered quite how she could know this. Somehow though she believed in her heart, it was truth.

"Please follow Oaklee," Ariella indicated a short Ilf with a serious face contrasting with her own warm, generous smile. It became clear though that he was not unfriendly simply honoured and intent on performing his task to solemn perfection. He bowed and walked circumspectly and, as with all Ilves, rapidly. Quickly leading the party into a leafy corridor, winding upwards into a vast tree with corridor-width boughs.

They followed him through a curtain of silver foliage with Grilvelline flower bells chiming as they brushed against them, releasing a delicate aroma, which filled their jangling senses with an indescribable calm. They soon found themselves in a leafy room. The ornate walls were made of fine interwoven silver branches, decorated with multicoloured leaves and draped with gossamer.

Ariella, following from the rear, said in a tinkling voice, "From the Goosemarren tree. You will see those in your travels, rare and inaccessible." She acknowledged Jenna's appreciation of the gossamer.

"So soft!" replied Jenna, unable to resist touching, "Like a kitten's fur."

"And warm," Ariella pointed out. "We have harsh winters. Please won't you sit down?" Her manner reminded Jenna of her sister as she indicated seats, also made of the gossamer, so comfy as they sank down into them. It was as though they had arrived home until Renewil blundered in through the curtain but as the aroma deepened they all laughed peaceably.

"Renewil! I have missed you. How are you?" Ariella spoke to the blushing owline, with great fondness in a language that none could understand except Jenna who was astounded to appreciate that she could also understand Renewil's reply.

"I missed you too. How is Gerelf?"

Ariella stroked him, fondly, as she answered, "Oh, you know him! Out hunting. But he won't be long." Until now, Jenna had not had chance to notice or appreciate Renewil because whilst he had been blundering around the group for some while, everyone had been too preoccupied with Emeriel's abduction and Methven's loss.

His feathers were the colour of a raven's on his head and wings, with a creamy breast, speckled black, and a pure white face like a dove. His wingspan was about Jenna's arm length. He had enormous, chestnut, owl-like eyes and could turn his head on his neck almost 180 degrees, and it could not be said that his clumsiness was due to poor visual abilities.

Ariella was still talking to him in Owline, "Do you have the Lore Book and the Jewel of Nilhspring with you?"

He nodded, blushing again. His snowy white cheeks and even his beak tinged a little. He lifted his wing and with his other, retrieved and presented the sizeable Lore Book to Ariella. Jish laughed as he watched the Chosen Ones' faces, he had seen Renewil's Gifft many times before.

Any ceremony demanding the presence of the Lore Book and therefore transportation from the Timewatcher's Tower required this Gifft. Justice had bestowed it upon Renewil in the Dawning. He then produced the Jewel of Nilhspring from behind his feathery pointed white ears. Jes was reminded of the Magician's trick he had seen at Jenna's last birthday party. The Jewel lay in an intricate silver box suitable to its task with the words:

Δανγερ ϑεωελ οφ Νιλησπρινγ Δο νοτ ρεμοϖε

engraved upon it in blood red letters.

Jes and Jenna had only heard mention of it until then but what they learned before peleve stayed with them forever. The Jewel could protect, guide and held enormous power. It could be a tool for great good but in Devlin hands would become a tool for evil. The Dreaded Race was trying to obtain the Jewel for its own wicked purposes.

The Lore Book contained the instructions for it's use and both were necessary to the Devlins to enable them to take control of Faerspring. If the Jewel were lost to Faerspring, the citizens would become mortal and die. Ariella explained to them that this would impact on their own world since the Faerspringians distant relatives, the Fairies, would no longer tend the plants and animals there as they had for aeons and their own World would degenerate and expire slowly. Jes felt rather cynical about this until Ariella patiently reminded him of his current origin.

As nel deepened, the Ancient Book of Lore and Flowers of Faerspring was opened. Ariella's face shone as she read to herself. The Lore was made of leather and the pages emitted a hazy golden glow as they were turned, lighting the room. The gathered company looked on in silent respect and when she looked up eventually her face held a sad smile and tears trickled down her fine boned cheeks.

She spoke after a while, "You must eat and then rest. The journey ahead will require courage and strength!"

All needed to ask, "But what did...?" And yet none of the assembled group could bring themselves to open their mouths; they were all too afraid to hear her reply, they knew that whatever had caused her such great sadness they must still journey on.

As Oaklee and his assistant Applebee prepared the meal, Ariella took Jes to one side and whispered in his ear, "May I see your arm Jes?" He was shocked because he had spoken to no one about it, not even to Emeriel or Jenna.

Ariella had seen him rubbing it every time the Devlins were mentioned. She looked thoughtfully at it and quietly pressed a decorated pot into his hand and said, "Use this. It will help with the pain, but be aware…you must heed its warnings when the time comes!"

He went to ask her what she meant but she put her fingers gently to his lips silencing him.

Oaklee and Applebee brought a perfunctory meal of delicious seed bread, both filling and warming. As they ate, it turned into liquid so there was no necessity for any drink to be served. After a few pieces, they all fell into a deeply refreshing sleep, including Torro and Renewil. There were many rooms in Ilvwood village; the kindly, proud inhabitants carried the tired guests in gossamer hammocks along the interlinked boughs, to their carefully prepared accommodation.

…And so, whilst Emeriel awoke in her prison cell, they woke to gossamer luxury following their best night's sleep ever, to the dawn chorus in Ilvwood, refreshed and ready for their travels. During the nel, each of them had been watched over by an assigned Ilf, dedicated to caring for them and keeping them safe. This meant that on waking they were greeted by a smiling Ilf, a quite disorientating experience for the Chosen Ones. They were presented with freshly laundered clothes and a snack-filled gossamer knapsack.

Once dressed, they were led to Ariella's suite of leafy rooms in the boughs of an enormous oak tree. She was resting on goose down cushions, embroidered with the finest gold thread, robed in a splendid gown of forest green silk.

Her hair had been elaborately plaited and wrapped in a coil, like a crown on her head, interwoven with delicate crimson rosaferbuds and tiny sparkling deep green gems. Jes was mesmerised. She was so beautiful. He remembered the pot she had given him and surreptitiously applied the sparkling paste within. It helped immediately. Jenna was too busy noticing that Ariella's belt, necklace and a bracelet matched perfectly, like a real princess.

"Did you sleep well, my friends?" She enquired. They nodded politely slightly in awe of her lovely presence. "Please sit." She beckoned them and her Ilf helpers provided cushions for them. "I have read and interpreted the Lore Book. Now I must tell you all you need to know to journey on."

There was silence as she continued. "You will need to travel to Faer Isle, the home of Princess Rhianne, my eldest sister. You will have to cross the Mountains of Dreadrock to get there speedily. You will need to take the Jewel with you for protection; without it, you will not survive the crossing.

"There is a portion of the Lore Book newly revealed which I cannot translate as it is in the Ancient Tongue of Faerderla. I believe Rhianne, is the only one who may help. Emeriel's whereabouts is contained within this passage. I have my suspicions about where she may be, but without a map and clear directions, even with the Jewel there would be grave danger. I hope the passage in Faerderla contains guidance for your safety."

She went on uncertainly, great concern in her voice. "I learned much from the chapter I could translate and will provide you with all that I can. I am not allowed to tell your future, it is written in the Lore, Justice has forbidden it.

"You must understand it is for good reason, since you may try and alter the future with the best of intentions but potentially at greater cost." Ariella became very solemn as she continued, "We must all play our part. I should make you aware that the final chapters of the Lore Book remain unwritten as yet. They will be revealed as Justice sees fit for our understanding and help."

Chapter Fifteen

The Mountains of Dreadrock

There were tears in Ariella's eyes, as she waved farewell from her balcony to the departing group making their way to the restless, fidgeting Loro. Jenna could not help but notice. She turned to Jes and asked doubtfully, "Why won't Ariella tell us what she read? If we knew, then, we could plan for it and it would help us, wouldn't it?"

Jes, who had been puzzling over the issue as well, replied confidently, "She would tell us if she could, I'm sure. But she seems to know that the consequences of that would be worse."

Jasper who had overheard Jenna's question added, "Justice is very powerful and separated the Devlins in the Awakening because they were so evil. In the beginning, Devlins were the same as any other Faerspringians but a group led by one named Drevilarche arose.

"He was unhappy and intent on upsetting the natural order. He wanted to be the Chief of Nilhspring, although it was not his right. Justice intervened, banishing his wicked band to Goth Devlin and over time they have become what they are now. Prior to this, all Faerspringians were mortal but since that event we are immortal."

He sounded authoritative and they listened intently as he elaborated further. "Because Jish and I are in the Timewatcher's Tower we know much of the Lore and our History. If Ariella told us what lies ahead and if something bad were meant to happen to one of us we would take alternative options in order to avoid what is written and change events. This would mean that the Final Chapter could have an awful ending. I think she is saying, if we follow the path, as it is already written, the Final Chapter will be as it should be."

"It is a bit complicated and worrying though?" Jenna queried again.

"No! We don't worry about the future. We try and fulfil our role to the best of our ability and trust Justice to reveal from the Lore what is needed. We know he has our best interests at heart."

"We don't know the future on earth, either." Jes said, with unusual insight.

By this time, they were packed and seated on Loro once more. Ariella continued waving. All the Ilves were present and wishing them a safe journey. The travellers departed on Loro smiling and waving back as they rose up through the leafy canopy, into the bright light of the suns' shine. Their smiles did not reveal their increasing inner dread of failure, especially without Methven. Jenna bit her lip and tried to be brave. She patted Loro in a friendly way, but she sought consolation.

Jish was preoccupied, initially with the motion of the Lorduress, but Renewil and Torro distracted and entertained him with a game of chase, though there was not a great deal room for it. It worked for a while but then nausea started sweeping over him again. Renewil communicated to Jenna that there was an Ilvish potion in Jish' knapsack, which would restore him. Following his instruction, she found a crystal bottle containing incandescent purple fluid.

"That's it!" Renewil said. Jes, observing this interaction, had not realised that Jenna had this Gifft and was amazed to see it in action. Jish took the potion and fell asleep immediately smiling and grateful.

Jes, Jenna and Jasper fell into deep discussion, with Jenna asking Jasper what he knew of Princess Rhianne. Jes, however, wanted to know about the Mountains of Dreadrock. Jasper told them all he knew; that the Mountains were greatly feared, the highest on the Faerspring world and many had died attempting to cross them on foot.

In the winter, they were completely snow covered even from the foothills, which were many Faermills from the peaks. In the summer, only the peaks and the passes between were covered with thick blankets of snow. Of Princess Rhianne, he knew only that she was reported to be even more beautiful than her two lovely sisters.

Jes found this hard to believe since, "Ariella was so especially lovely."

This statement led to much noisy teasing and joking, causing Jish to waken. When Jenna helpfully shared the joke with him he laughed until he cried. The potion was clearly helping, as he felt quite well enough to join in the fun, adding to Jes' embarrassment. They had no concept of the journey's length but soon understood it would be longer than the last.

After many Faermills of faithful flapping, Jenna felt Loro tiring and she stroked his hard scaly neck. She spoke directly to him in Lordurian. She was developing her Gifft, and finding ways to utilise it to benefit everyone. Loro acknowledged her kindness, with a small puff of smoke. He was too exhausted to talk, at the moment. Jenna recognised that; she was learning a great deal about the Lorduress. When he was tired, his wings flapped heavily with a thudding quality. She wondered if the conscientious Ilves would have considered provisions for Loro and concluded there would be refreshment for him.

She gently nudged Jasper who was dozing next to the backpacks and softly asked him to look. He rummaged through the packs sleepily and found a parcel wrapped in fine linen with Loro's name embroidered in gold thread. As Jasper passed it to her drowsily, she marvelled at the diligence and thoughtfulness of their hosts the previous nel. She had felt so peaceful there.

Unwrapping the package with extreme care, she found small linen pouches tied with golden, intertwined, leaf string. Each pouch was labelled, though she could not read the letters, as they were indistinct except one clearly stating, "Loro Feed". She opened it and found a mixture of dried fruit, seeds and nuts.

Loro had a keen sense of smell and his nostrils twitched appreciatively as he twisted his neck around at a most peculiar angle. She reached as far forward as she could, enabling him to eat from her outstretched hand, just! The resulting wild nose-dive caused a great deal of commotion, alarming Jish considerably. However, Jenna's intuition had proved correct and though it was only a small handful, he continued on his way with renewed vitality and enthusiasm.

Finally, Jenna too, drifted off to sleep. It was nelfall and many Faermills later, when Jes woke from his dreams with a start. He was confused, unsure where he was or why he had woken, but then he realised the scar was causing him extreme pain.

He reached into his tunic for the pot and then remembered Ariella's words as the pain intensified he knew something terrible and evil was occurring. He saw the foothills of the Mountains of Dreadrock below. He shouted to waken everyone as Loro's flight became more erratic as he darted around.

"Hold tight!" Jes yelled, grabbing Jenna despite his searing pain. The violent movements became even more pronounced as Loro did a steep perpendicular drop angled sharply to the right. The others were now wide awake and hanging on for dear life.

The startled and petrified Jasper was peering around in the gloom and became aware of tens of dark-winged forms surrounding Loro, with huge fangs and jagged wedge-shaped ears, black with the exception of their ferocious-looking crimson heads. In close proximity, Jenna knew they were attempting to bite Loro. He was petrified and quivering, but was valiantly trying to avoid them.

"We must try and help him!" She yelled, above the noise of their flapping wings and high-pitched squeaking. As the creatures flocked around poor Loro, Renewil caught a glimpse of the terrifying vamplins, remembering them from a previous encounter.

"If one sinks its' fangs into Loro's scales he will be injected with an immobilising potion and that'll be us!" He told Jenna. She relayed the news to Jes, who had recognised the evil creatures from his own encounter. His arm was seizing up rapidly and, awkwardly using his left hand, he undid the pot and applied the paste as rapidly as he could. The relief was instant.

"What can we do?" Jes queried, desperately looking toward Jasper. In that instant, Renewil took off and they watched him, mouths open in horror, as he deftly flew amongst the appalling vamplins. They pursued him, distracted from their previous target. Renewil spun, dived and disappeared into the damp, distant darkness. Loro flew bravely on toward the snow-covered peaks as he regained his sense of direction. Slowly his shocked trembling lessened.

Jenna stifled a sob rising in her throat, as she realised that Renewil might have sacrificed his life for their safety. Silence fell as they gazed back into the horrible void into which Renewil had sped. It was some time before the deathly hush was broken.

"Should we eat something?" Jes whispered, in subdued tones to Jasper, who replied with a solemn nod of his head. The sad group passed around their backpacks and opened them. Each found a number of linen pouches like Loro's. One had the word, "Food" embroidered on it. It was the only legible pouch.

They ate the Ilve Bread without a word passing between them but it filled them with hope and renewed their forlorn spirits. They each had a named silver flask and finished the meal off with this. It was sweet and syrupy and unbelievably refreshing. Loro was flagging anew, especially after the vamplin attack and Jenna revived him with another mouthful of his feed. Jish readied himself this time.

Eventually they found themselves flying across the peaks of the Mountains of Dreadrock, accompanied by a ferocious storm with lightening unlike any thing they had witnessed before. The Mountains looked fearsome enough, but when the electric brightness lit the sky they were even more overwhelming and frightening. It was not difficult to see that Ariella had been speaking the truth.

Loro struggled bravely on but was forced to fly low to avoid the worst of the storm. This caused them to be alarmingly close to the mountains. Narrowly missing jutting edges of rock, he brushed so close to the snowy peaks on occasions, that he started dramatic cascading avalanches.

As the storm raged on, his left wing tipped a particularly prominent ledge, which sent them all spiralling downwards in a vortex. The group were desperately clinging on as Loro toppled, spinning and against all odds he managed to crash-land on a snowy precipice over a bottomless crevasse. They were dazed and shocked.

Loro's wing was badly gashed and bleeding profusely, though the others had only bruises and minor cuts. Loro had made sure he minimised the impact for them but at great cost to himself. The injury was deep and Jasper, who knew much of the Herbal Lore Medicine, suspected it might be fatal.

Jenna knew too from Loro's soft moaning that it was serious. Torro nuzzled his neck and Loro's eye opened and then, fluttered shut. They leapt down as quickly and gently as they could. The wind was biting. The ice, underfoot, chilling. Loro's blood now made a horrifying crimson red pool on the pure snow.

"The back pack," Jes barked sharply as Jasper assessed the wound. Jish looked around in vain; even he was upset to see Loro like this, after the way he had worked so selflessly for them. Jenna searched with him and then noticed it was lying on the other side of the crevasse. Jenna lamented Renewil's absence as he could have flown across. She was desperate to save Loro.

"Please do something Jes!" Jenna begged her brother. He felt helpless but then as he was gazing in earnest at the backpack it shifted fractionally, he concentrated intensely and remembering his fledgling Gifft he transported it safely back across the crevasse.

Jenna delved into the pack and found a linen pouch, labelled in gold embroidered letters, "Healing Balm". She deftly opened the wrapper to reveal a blue gel pulsating in a crystal ampoule.

Jasper said, "Heaserum nectar, an ancient Ilve Herb. It stings intensely when applied to a wound, but has cleansing and healing properties. Jenna can you comfort him while I apply it?" He unloosened the lid carefully and using the gossamer pad in the pouch, applied it with great tenderness to the gaping wound on the underside of his wing, as Jenna whispered Lordurian into Loro's ear, cradling him.

In her distress, she had not even realised that she had used his ancient tongue and clearly had the Gifft of speaking in his language as well as being able to understand it. They looked on with great concern as the gel pulsated and swelled to fill the wound stemming the blood flow at the same time.

"There's no more we can do for him now. We can only wait." Jasper sighed, resigned and helpless like the rest. Loro shifted slightly, snorting gently as he lifted his head and then collapsed back into the drifting icy snow. He would not be able to go any further and, as the suns dawned, the weary, despondent pilgrims found themselves atop the peaks of the mountains, cold and alone, with their only means of escape and survival lying unconscious and in critical danger.

Renewil's return at that precise moment was miraculous, causing a mighty cheer and much backslapping. Torro performed acrobatics, including expert claw stands and back flips, in his ecstasy. Renewil alighted next to Loro's head with evident concern; a tear appeared and slid down his white cheek. Jenna explained what had happened.

Pelfirst was a chilly affair and they dipped deeper into their supplies and flasks. Another pouch had become legible now, "For warmth". Shivering, they all acknowledged this must be the moment and Jes delved into the pouch. He unwrapped a tiny, neatly packed gossamer blanket puzzling in its size until it was unfolded and expanded rapidly to provide a thick woven covering, sufficient for them all to snuggle under providing they huddled close together, next to Loro.

Jenna was worried about Loro's welfare though and knew he was cooling quickly. She rummaged and discoverd another pouch, with "Loro's warmth" now visible on it. They covered him with it, despite a fierce struggle against the howling gale, and huddled under it tent-style, close to Loro to keep him warm. The storm raged outside and Renewil recounted to Jenna how he had led the vamplins into a huge cave and then used his body cloaking gift to escape the evil hoards, while she translated his tale for the others. They fell into silent sadness, as Loro's breathing became shallower and less frequent, his condition deteriorating rapidly.

Chapter Sixteen

Emeriel's Lesson

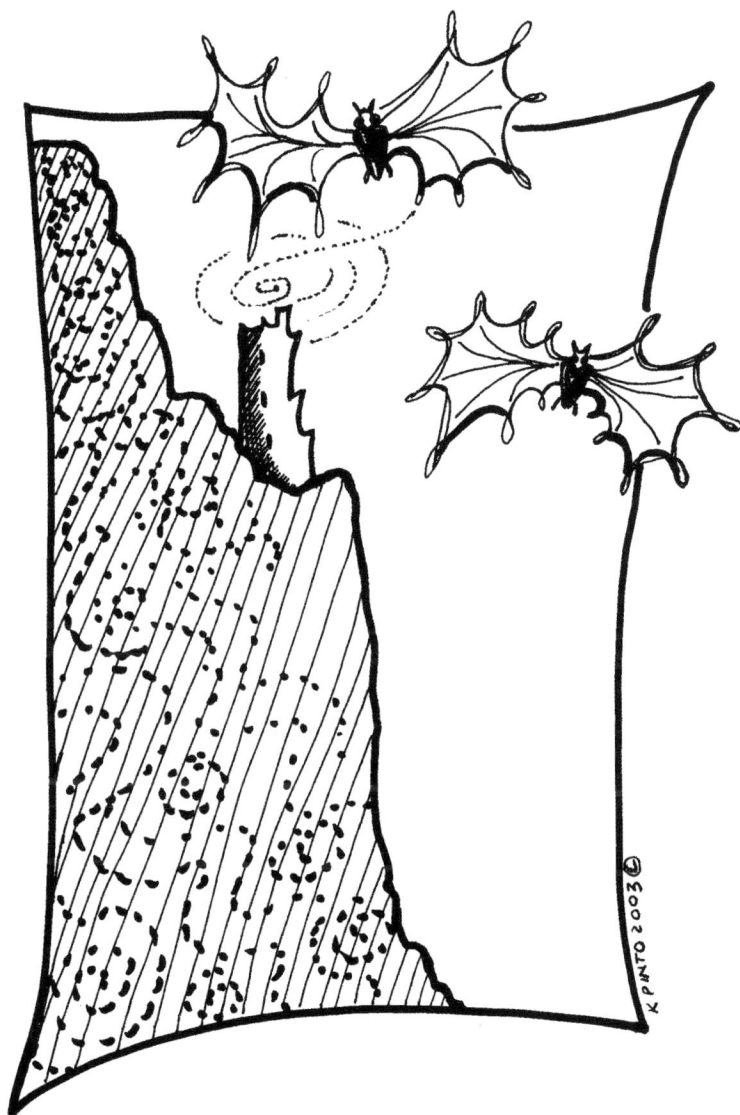

Emeriel could have done with a few lessons from Renewil on the subject of body cloaking, having spent the last pel and nel, trying to flip in and out. It was really quite a problem since she was perched on the narrow ledge, not knowing where or how to go. From the time Lord Madded and Brendded had scuttled off, she had been trying to find some escape route but despite her frantic searching she could see no way down the cliff. It was a sheer drop on three sides and on the fourth side cliffs rose steeply above the Fortress. Huge bat-like creatures wheeled overhead circling the Tower, Emeriel noted their crimson heads and tried to recall where she had seen them before.

She made several attempts to climb the intimidating cliffs but, having nearly lost her footing twice, decided it was far too dangerous and, besides, she could see that the mountain range beyond was impassable. Various Devlins had already passed her and she was learning that they had a particularly foul odour in close proximity; body cloaking offered her no protection from this vile fact. She was finding it very difficult to body cloak as and when needed, noting on occasions that one or other of her feet was still visible, but as well as being of low intellect she was learning that Devlins were fortunately not particularly observant either.

Pelfirst found her cold and hungry, with a dawning realisation that, at some point soon, she would need to go back underground to find food. The next passing Devlin happened to be Brendded and she followed him invisibly, through a door, which led down into the subterranean passages and corridors. As they descended they moved nearer to the thudding. She wondered anew what this could be. She was tempted to go off and explore but was too hungry to risk becoming lost and decided the safest option was to continue following Brendded in the hope that he would be returning to the prison area. Also, in a moment of inspiration she decided that if she could contact Anuthel, he might be able to help.

Her hope proved correct and before long Brendded was setting out across the dim courtyard and since she was following this time, rather than being pushed from behind, she had a better opportunity to look around. There was no natural light and the courtyard actually had a ceiling so high above it was indistinguishable. She noticed that the prison was built into the walls of an enormous cavern. She could hear bats, catching glimpses of them sporadically and noting their unusual heads with razor sharp fangs. Occasionally she saw huge stalactites, jutting down into the cavern from far above. There were two identical doors on opposite walls. Brendded approached one, keys jangling as he unlocked it. She nipped in quickly before he closed it again and found herself in a room full of Devlins sitting at long benches with large tankards on the tables. She was terrified as they grunted at each other and scuffles and tussles broke out amongst them. It was extremely, unpleasant; both smelly and hot.

She was relieved when she overheard Brendded talking about having to go, as he was on the next prison shift. She hoped it would be on Anuthel's corridor although she had no idea what else may be within the building. She followed him closely, trembling uncontrollably as she did not want to be discovered and find herself back in that awful cell. She thought she remembered the corridor but was unsure until she recognised the ugly blood splash on the floor. She watched Brendded, hearing his thoughts, as he checked each cell carefully, making sure there were no other escapees. He had really got into a pile of trouble after that Faerspringian had escaped; he would not chance another.

Emeriel waited patiently, hoping he would not be long. Body cloaking was draining her reserves rapidly and, although inexperienced, she sensed she would not be able to affect it for much longer. As soon as he was gone she rushed over to Anuthel's cell door. She tried thought speech, but to no avail this time. "What now?" She wondered. The key was hanging by the door but what if he'd been moved and anyway how did she know if she could trust him? She had felt she could. While debating the issue, she forgot about body cloaking and, unhappily for her, Brendded made an unexpected reappearance. He could not believe his good fortune when he spied her. He grabbed her roughly by the arms, thrusting her into the empty cell with great delight.

She was shocked. Devastated. It would be much harder to make another escape now they were aware of her body cloaking ability. She sobbed, huddled against the wall.

"Emeriel! Is that you?" She heard thought speech, from the next cell.

"Anuthel?"

"Yes! What happened?"

"I'll tell you. But first, you tell me, who and what you are?" Emeriel was feeling miserable, suspicious and not in the mood for any further disasters. Thought blocking, to avoid divulging information to the enemy, any enemy, she asked, "And why you are here?"

"I'm sorry. Forgive me! Anuthel the Ancient, a Dwarf of Dwindell, near Nilhspring at your service." He replied, with a softer tone to his thought for he was feeling sorry for her.

"How do you know my name?"

"You are one of the Chosen Ones. It is written in the Lore."

"The Lore Book? What do you know of it?" She was beginning to feel he was friend not foe, but needed to be sure.

"We have a copy of it, under close guard, deeply hidden in the Caves of Antiquaria in the Mountains of Wisdom. You need not fear, Emeriel, our meeting is foretold."

She logically supposed, that if he was locked up too, he must be on the same side.

"If it's foretold, you'll be able to tell me when we get out of here, then?"

"That I may not say, but get out we will. First, we have much to do here."

"There's not much to do in my cell."

"I mean we have a task to accomplish here in this wicked place. Goth Malin harbours great evil, as I'm sure you have realised. We must end it!"

"Yes! All well and good, but there's not much likelihood of that at present unless you know how to pass through walls." She continued, laughing, her sense of humour returning now that she had found an ally.

"As a matter of fact, I do," he replied airily. "But we will need to teach you a thing or two!"

And so began, Emeriel's lessons in body cloaking through solid objects, which she found very frustrating and exhausting. Together they spent the best part of the next pel and nel with her bumping head long into the wall; she was covered in bruises before eventually she sarcastically said, "Why don't you come through here and demonstrate, if it's so easy?"

"OK!" He whispered in her right ear, giving her quite a start. She had not realised how rapidly passing through walls could be achieved.

"Neat trick!" she whispered back. "Any chance of meeting you in the flesh?"

Instantly, the diminutive but impressive, brown caped figure of Anuthel the Ancient appeared. He was shorter than Emeriel, even with his pointed hat of woven amber cloth taken into account, and it stood at least an arms length above him. He had a long white beard reaching to a leather belt encompassing his stout waist, though waist implies a narrowing and in Anuthel's case there was more of a widening at that point. He had piercing dark-blue eyes on either side of a bulbous red nose. She couldn't help but like the chubby fellow. In his roughened hand, he held a wooden staff. Though humble in it's appearance she was later to learn its awesome capabilities.

"Anuthel the Ancient!" he smiled formally, bowing perfunctorily. "I rather like you, too," he added, his belly wobbling gleefully. Emeriel had accidentally let the thought block slip, in her surprise.

"Now, back to business!" He tapped his staff sharply on her head, as she disappeared. He grasped her arm firmly and muttered. "Now off we go!" He prodded her with the wooden staff and though she felt extremely annoyed at being pushed, nevertheless, through the wall they went into his cell.

Suddenly on the dark corridor outside they were aware of the heavy thud of Devlin footsteps and the key turning in the lock of Anuthel's cell door.

"Don't worry," she heard him, silently. "They are not renowned for their memories. He won't notice or remember which cell we were in. Anyway we don't have the time to sort it. Just look relaxed."

"Easier thought than done," she mused urgently trying to de-body cloak. He coolly disappeared back into the other cell. She assumed a blank expression and looked directly at the blundering, agitated Devlin, Bigeviledd this time, who really appeared, none the wiser. He was certainly alarmed at the prospect of her doing another 'runner'. He quickly put the bread and water on the cold floor, and still facing Emeriel, he exited, beetling backwards with remarkable speed for a Devlin.

The process was repeated for Anuthel and each of the other prisoners. Emeriel wondered for the first time who else was locked up with them and she heard Anuthel's silent, "Mostly criminal Devlins! Though quite how they tell the difference I'm sure I can't tell."

"Quite! 'Cos they're not all locked up here. But, they're all criminal, aren't they?" Emeriel echoed.

"Actually, pretty much so! But there are some good ones, I've known a few but that's a story for another pel. Right! He's gone now. Back to the lessons! Let's eat first, I'm starving."

"You don't look starved to me," Emeriel thought quietly, again forgetting the thought block.

"Watch it!" he responded defensively, but in good part.

"I'm tired." She sighed.

"So am I. Now. You've seen how it's done. You've done it with me. Just do it yourself. You come and visit me? Of course, you might be a slow learner; I've had a few of them in my time. I remember…"

"Why you miserable, good for nothing, Dwarf!" she thought, though whether she was more annoyed at being called a slow learner or the thought of another Dwarf story. Before she knew it she was back in her own cell again waving her finger furiously at him. Her rage intensified at the sight of him rolling around rotundly on her cell floor.

"You did it!" He yelled, delightedly and audibly!

"Shush! We'll get caught!"

"Aaahh! But, can you do it again?" He challenged, gleaming eyes full of doubt and mischief.

"Of course!" she said angrily, bumping with a painful thud into the wall yet again, "Ouch!

"Concentrate!"

"Stop ordering me about, would you?" She felt exceedingly irritated with him as she sailed through the wall, unhindered and body cloaked. "I did it! I did it!"

"Ok! Ok! We are rolling now!" he said in a quaint Dwarfish way, though it reminded her of something else.

Meanwhile, Bigevileddd was puzzling over his prison cell map in confusion. It was his job as the supervisor to see that the next shift had a clearly written, well at least, drawn, plan. Being illiterate and deprived of any real memory, they relied on symbols. "Faerspringian…Dwarf… Devlin…" And he had spent some while deciphering the symbols and felt sure something was amiss, so off he trotted to check once more. He'd seen poor old Brendded with one ear lobe hanging off and the way his knee now bent the other way. He stomped back to the third floor, noisily checking each cell.

Emeriel and Anuthel convulsed with laughter in their respective cells, stifling their giggles at his slow lengthy ponderings. Made funnier by knowing exactly what the other was thinking. Finally Emeriel's laughter erupted explosively with a loud hiss. Even Bigeviledd, deep in slow thought, heard it and decided to unlock the door to check.

"OK! Emi, it's now or never, let's go!!" Anuthel's thought sounded so informal, but she was beginning to recognise his brand of humour. She looked at the door and concentrated hard on trying to feel afraid enough to body cloak, nothing happened, but thankfully Anuthel grabbed her hand with, "C'mon, you silly Faerie, cut the nonsense. Through the wall!"

Chapter Seventeen

Loro The Brave

Meanwhile as the snowstorm raged outside the other Chosen Ones sheltered despite certain knowledge of their hopeless and grim predicament. Renewil was almost instantly asleep as he tucked his head down into his chest and dreamt about avoiding giant vamplins. Jes and Jish dropped off to sleep huddled against Loro's fading hulk; Jes was clutching his stiff aching arm, too tired to bother with the healing paste. Jasper and Jenna each sat in quiet desperation wondering what they might do to help and if they couldn't…

Tears trickled slowly down Jenna's pale, frightened face as she whispered in Lordurian. Torro snuggled close to Loro's side, devastated at the possibility of losing his greatest friend.

Jasper shrieked suddenly, "The Lore Book!! Jenna wake Renewil! We need the Lore!" Jenna wasn't about to argue, they certainly needed something. She gently shook Renewil out of his nightmare, waking him with a start. He took the Lore from under his wing and passed it to Jasper drowsily, without a sound and promptly fell asleep again.

"How does he do that?" Jenna asked, her interest distracting her.

"Typical Owline, always asleep when you need them."

"We have a bird just like that on earth but they sleep with one eye open!"

"Aaah well, back in the Awakening, before all the trouble with mortality, that's how Owline were. They were renowned for their observational skills, but it all changed. Renewil is actually quite good. Some of them are barely ever awake! Never mind that, this may be our way out." Jasper replied, with a confidence he did not, in truth possess.

Nervously and with great respect he unfastened the Lore indicating no one should speak. He scanned the antique parchment pages carefully. He was sure there was a passage pertaining to healing requests in dire situations of importance to the fabric of Faerspringian life. At last he found the Writt of Healing and read about the Angel of Justice.

He read the text several times until he could repeat the petition word perfect. As instructed, he knelt, hung his head and repeated the ancient words,

"ϑυστιχε, I ιμπλορε τηεε

Ασ I βενδ μψ κνεε

Μαψ τηε Αενγελ

Χομε ανδ ηεαλ

Λορο τηε Βραϖε"

He waited then, believing he would be heard, although he did not know what the answer might be. Truth be told, he was petrified that the Angel of Justice would come, as he had heard many ancient tales about the power the Angel possessed.

At this moment he rather hoped they were myths and not facts, but deep down he knew this was Loro's only chance. He also knew that Loro's death would mean they would all perish on these Mountains, and that Faerspring would fall under the control of unspeakable evil.

Jenna stirred. She sensed Loro's demise was imminent. His breathing rattled in frequent short gasps. Desolation at what seemed an inevitable loss overwhelmed her.

Just as she stirred, a bolt of lightening tore the shelter asunder and bathed them in such intense white dazzling light that they all awoke abruptly and immediately had to shield their eyes. They could hear a rushing sound, like a wild sweeping wind and the sound of wings beating.

Then a powerful voice spoke with authority, the noise like the tremendous roar of a thousand waterfalls,

"Λορο ρισε. ϑυστιχε ηασ νεεδ οφ ψου. Ιτ ισ νοτ ψουρ τιμε ψετ."

Jasper knew, with certainty, it was the Angel. He tried to open his eyes but was blinded by the light's intensity. He felt a gentle touch on his shoulder. A feeling of peace filled his fearfully disturbed mind.

Jish had also read of the rare miraculous visits and though it had not happened for millennia he also recognised that they were in the presence of the Angel of Justice. He lacked the courage to try to look at the awesome being but nevertheless felt honoured to be present.

Jes realised in utter disbelief that his arm had stopped aching and was astonished to see that the scar had vanished completely but he now had a tiny blue mark, which was glowing faintly. Jenna was in a state of abject terror and shock but it was such a brief moment.

When they later discussed the occurrence, they were both frustrated by their inability to describe it. They even doubted it had taken place at all. Still without question from that moment onward Loro slowly revived, regaining his strength.

He returned to consciousness at midpel, giving his now sleeping companions a rude awakening in the process. Jasper knew from the Lore that a Visitation always resulted in those visited falling into a long, deep sleep.

They were delighted to see his snorting nostrils and twinkling eyes; the complete destruction of the shelter was irrelevant, compared to his return to full health. They looked out at the twilight and suns setting in the distance over the seas, realising the storm had abated and the snow was heaped up around them. Loro began to shiver.

"Does anyone know how we can warm Loro up?" Jenna enquired with concern. "He's so cold!" She whispered sensitively to him in Lordurian. "You're cold. How can we warm you?" She was so delighted to have him to fuss over.

Loro chortled, snorting out a few bright flames from his nostrils. The snow in front of him melted and he chuckled as he drank the puddle he had created. He worked his way around, creating a small clearing on the icy peak.

It took a while but he whistled cheerfully until the freezing group were standing on a dry glassy area, albeit slightly sizzled in places.

As the suns finally set, Jish delved inside the ever fruitful knap sacks and found a parcel labelled "Fuel". Loro happily snorted a few flames to light the fuel and soon they were camping by a warm fire, under the moons and stars, cooking food in a pot from the knapsacks.

"The way the writing is becoming legible as we go, is a bit spooky isn't it? And it's always exactly what we need." Jenna said to Jes.

Jish overheard and answered, "We'd call it Ilvish Providence!" He pulled out another linen package, labelled, "New Shelter" which they re-established, settling to eat their delicious Hot Thistleberry Stew accompanied by Crillis and Emerene. Ilvish Providence was rather welcome at this point.

"Jasper this is fantastic how do the Ilves know the future like this?" Jes asked.

Pleased to be asked, Jasper responded, "Simple. Ariella studied the Lore Book, didn't she? Don't forget, this was foretold. They would have been very busy packing for our journey. Only Justice knows the future but the Lore tells of important events for Faerspring. It was written down by the Priests of Ruthrigalis after the Awakening, under Justice' direction."

It all sounded fascinating but once they had eaten their hot meal with Emerene, they were so relaxed they fell back into deep slumber. Jes was the last to succumb as he gazed up at the stars contemplating which constellation could conceivably contain Earth…. and Grandma's home.

Early before pellight, they roused. Much of the previous peleve seemed like a dream to them. They felt dazed and amazed, Jes and Jenna, in particular, were disbelieving. Loro seemed so full of life but an enthusiastic, happy Lorduress was a liability on a snowy mountain peak and they quickly packed, disturbing the slothful Renewil to ensure both the Jewel and Lore Book were still safe. They departed without any further delay and with great relief. Loro's wing had healed. Only a most observant and sensitive Faerspringian would have noticed a slight weakness on his left wing and Jenna comforted him and encouraged him. She began to sing to him as she often did with injured animals:

"Loro the Brave, Loro the Great

You have overcome your Fate,

You are wise! You are strong!

We will sing the whole pel long!"

Jes wanted to laugh and unfortunately caught Jish trying to stifle a giggle. Jasper looked sternly at them both, but their attempts to avoid laughing were infectious and he ended up joining them. Jenna would have been quite upset, but Loro was swaying gracefully and appreciatively to her song and soon the others were joining in, adding verses of their own.

The most amusing was a contribution from Jes:

"Jish the sorry, Jish the sick

Loro can he get there quick!

Jish is green, Jish is white!

And we know he loves this flight!"

Even Jish thought it funny, fortunately he had taken some of the Ilvish remedy earlier, otherwise he might not have. Many verses followed, the most poignant being:

"Emi the Lost, Emi the Brave,

On our way, for you to save,

It will be hard; it will be soon,

We will fly beneath the gloom."

Jasper wondered whether in yers to come, the verses, too many to note here, would be sung by future Faerspringian generations and be recorded in the Songs of the Lore as was customary to remind Faerspring of a great and tragic journey; or would they be unsuccessful and forgotten forever?

On they sped, over land and then sea covering many thousands of Faermills. Encouraged by Jenna, Loro headed for the Faer Isle. He knew where he was going even in the darkest nel, it was as though he had a compass in his tail, Jenna thought, patting him proudly.

Topel though, there was bright suns shine and a clear unclouded view, Loro could see where he was headed and so could Jenna. When she saw a distant island, with its glistening castle of many high turrets, she knew it was Faer Isle. She pointed it out to the others who had eventually dozed off, having exhausted themselves by the singing, despite their initial misgivings about it.

As they approached the island, they could see golden streams and waterfalls weaving amongst undulating hills and valleys. The castle rose majestically. Windows of multi-coloured glass in different shapes; round, square, hexagonal, hearts, and even wing shaped which glistened like mirrors. The walls sparkled in the midpel suns. As they neared they could see they were inlaid with crystals and precious stones in the marble.

"Its beautiful, isn't it?" Jenna murmured awestruck.

The castle itself was hexagonal with a large translucent door at the end of a rampart with brightly coloured flowers and neatly trimmed trees standing in pots and tubs. Within the walls was a stunning garden surrounding a gold shimmering pond. They were so distracted by the amazing sight they had not noticed that Loro was intent on landing on a high tower on the opposite side of the castle.

"It doesn't look Lorduress-size, Loro!" yelled Jes, suddenly realising the chosen landing spot. But with great agility, wings and back legs outstretched, Loro landed almost vertically like a hawk intent upon trapping a tasty mouse. The riders had heard Jes' warning and clung tightly to each other and the saddle. They were learning and this time they successfully avoided the usual crumpled heap fiasco.

The tower was made of pink and white chequered marble. Jenna was speechless at this Faerie Princess' Castle. She gazed around in amazement gasping and was the first to notice Princess Rhianne standing next to Loro;

she had appeared from nowhere.

Jasper and Jish gaped and performed a Faerspring bow, complete with transflight and the low dip appropriate to her status, but both blushed furiously. They were overwhelmed by her. Jasper managed, after a few stuttering moments, to recover his composure sufficiently to say, "Your Highness!"

As he took in the golden flowing ringlets reaching her ankles and her slender figure, he decided that whilst she was truly lovely, for him she did not compare with Ariella who appeared less distant and somehow warmer. Jenna noticed the dark blue eyes of the Princess; like the sea on a sunny day, and the full, rosy, red lips against purest alabaster skin. She looked so delicate and frail.

The travellers were quite surprised when they heard her commanding, clipped voice, "You're here! Welcome! Please, with me!" She swept her dainty hand around in a circle as a cloud of pink smoke engulfed them and they found themselves transported to a vast hexagonal hall with a black and white chequered floor and luscious smooth pink marble walls. Even Loro seemed tiny, within this room with its enormous, pastel-tinted, stained glass windows, letting delicate colour and light flood in.

She waved her hand again and chairs suddenly appeared. "Sit! The Lore Book, Renewil! No time to waste." Introductions were unnecessary it seemed. Jenna could not like the sharp tone this Princess used to address Renewil. Rhianne read silently, with no sign of emotion on her face. She glanced up and Jes was struck by her physical similarity to Ariella and Zithanduel, but also by her lack of emotion and curtness.

Jes did not like her either. Jasper warmly remembered the tears flooding down Ariella's lovely cheeks as she had read and decided that Rhianne could not compare. Jish was so stunned by her strict authority he was incapable of thought at all.

She continued to read as though they did not exist and then, proclaimed, "You need Jeruthel. He will help you get to Goth Malin. Emeriel and Anuthel are there!" and promptly disappeared.

Jes was furious, "Is that it? Who is Jeruthel? Where is Goth Malin? Who is Anuthel?" He was desperate to find Emeriel and now this overbearing Princess, who obviously knew exactly where she was, had disappeared as though it didn't matter.

"I thought Ariella said there would be a map and guidance." He turned angrily toward Jasper and Jish as though somehow it was their fault. "Well?"

Neither answered. Rhianne reappeared armed with a mace and a crystal sphere, wearing a gem-studded crown. "Right! Silence!" she snapped business-like at Jes and from the smouldering look on her pretty face it was evident she was aware of his words.

She struck the crystal and a golden aura emanated from her and the sphere. The Hall began to shift and shimmer, revolving around them. It rotated faster and faster, whilst they remained still and motionless, until it vanished.

They were on a glass platform in broken clouds, sea below, with two islands visible. She pointed to a dark mountainous island to the Nilh, "Goth Malin," and to the Silh, she pointed to another, which they guessed to be Faer Isle before she said it. Then, she showed them a stretch of water between the land and Goth Malin, "The Straight of Goth Aref." She pointed to a promontory, "The Ferry".

She waved her hand and they knew something dramatic was about to occur. This time the clouds and platform vanished and they found themselves floating above a dark fortress surrounded by fierce seas and steep cliffs. "Emeriel and Anuthel are, there, in the Fortress of Goth Devlin."

As she spoke Jes became aware of an almost imperceptible tingling in his arm where the wound had been and as he glanced at the tiny mark he realised with a start that it was now pulsing black not its previous blue. He was fearful.

"Take us there then!" Jes replied sharply but with a note of pleading.

"Yes and we can rescue them, please!" Jenna begged. But the hand of authority, waved anew and they were back in the imposing Hall.

"That is not possible. You should not ask." She answered with a stern rebuke.

"B..B..But." Jenna tried to argue, however Rhianne was clearly furious at being challenged and sat down abruptly tapping the crystal gently with the mace. A featureless face enshrouded in a dark cloak appeared dimly in the golden glow.

"Jeruthel, we need your help." She spoke in a gentler voice, reminding Jasper of Ariella. "The Chosen Ones are here. They must reach Goth Devlin!"

"I will help Princess, in return for a small favour…" He paused.

"Yes, yes…" She was impatient with him.

"When the Chosen Ones are finished their quest, I have need of the one called Loro." They each straightened up and looked around uncertainly, especially Loro and Torro.

"Fine! It is done. Now Jeruthel, I have the Key to the Ferry, will you permit its use?"

"Provided you keep you promise!" He retorted and in a flash he was gone.

There was silence.

"The Princess bargained with Loro without a second thought, and we are to cross the sea on a Ferry with a dark-hooded menacing blackmailer," thought Jes. "Just great!"

Jenna however was thinking, "We'll see about that. I'm not going to let her do that to Loro!"

"Ooh! No!… Not a boat" Jish only had his seasickness in mind. Boats were a great source of worry. Jasper could only anxiously think of Goth Devlin and all he had read of it in the Lore. Their mixed reactions merged to form an emphatic joint response and a loud, definite, "NO!!" followed by harmonious silence.

Nevertheless, Princess Rhianne simply turned and rapped, "You heard. You rest here for one nel. At pellight, you depart for the Ferry."

A sullen, hush followed as they considered their response but none spoke. Certainly not one of them would leave Loro, even Jish, as a favour for anyone or anything, but after the previous reaction from Rhianne there was little benefit debating the issue at this moment. The Princess had shown no sign of the Gifft of thought knowledge yet she knew their thoughts precisely and would take no account of them. They were quite right not to argue with her, as it would make no difference.

They spent a surprisingly pleasant peleve in the castle. Princess Rhianne commanded a feast, her servants appearing speedily and using all manner of Giffts to comply with her demands. Tables, chairs, Crillis, Emerene and other delicious, exotic dishes burst forth from nowhere. Tables and walls were decorated with flowers: pale silver Duckberry flowers, tiny Rall Tulps and Great Dairiels.

Jasper wondered at the way Giffts were used so readily here on Faer Isle, having been taught by 'Twit' to use them sparingly, only when essential. But if he wanted to ask why, he knew now was not the time and made a mental note to ask later.

Conversation revolved around the history of Faer Isle, Rhianne's voice held a note of previously unforeseen enthusiasm as she told them of the lives of King Faerutha and Queen Faerella and their daughters, Rhianne, Ariella and Zithanduel before the Faerspring world had become immortal. The Castle, from which Rhianne now ruled over Faerspring, had originally been their home.

With great animation she told of how Drevilarche murdered the King and Queen leaving the three sisters to fend for themselves and each other, in his effort to obtain Nilhspring and become the leader and take control of the Jewel. From the time of the monarch's grisly end Justice punished Drevilarche by handing Nilhspring to the Dwarves, one of the other inhabitants of Faerspring, for it's safekeeping. They were to guard it all cost.

Jenna politely asked Rhianne, "Please could you tell me why Justice made everyone immortal and where the children are?"

"Drevilarche was banished to the Nether World and his followers were scattered over the cold, dark lands beyond Nilhspring. Justice rewarded the rest of Faerspring with immortality to bring stability, following the loss of the King and Queen..." Her eyes misted over and she had difficulty holding her usually well-controlled emotions in check.

She went on brusquely, "And also because the Ilves had long sought immortality. Madded took over as Leader of Drevilarche's disbanded group and over time he regrouped them at Goth Malin. It was he who systematically poisoned the children of our races. We don't know how but we suspect he put something toxic to them only into the springs. Now he plots to overturn the natural order once more."

Jenna looked puzzled, "If you are immortal how can your children be poisoned? Surely you live and survive the poisoning?"

Rhianne smiled for the first time since they had arrived. "You are clever and astute, Jenna, wise for your yers. Those who live under the Lore and are poisoned or fatally wounded in battle are taken to the Land Beyond. We are free from ailments and ageing though. We are not able to reach those in the Land Beyond, who are with Justice, but they do live on, immortal indeed.

"Dragon Lore tells much of the Lorduress and the Lorduress minor. Before the Dawn of Immortality, they were numerous on Faerspring. They courageously defended the races of Faerspring against Drevilarche and his followers, but many were lost in the great battles. Now only a few remain in Ruthragon. Without their sacrificial fight, we would not be here now."

She acknowledged Loro, dozing dangerously near an open fireplace. He opened one lazy, fluidous eye at hearing his kin mentioned and solemnly winked at her. "The Jewel of Nilhspring was given to the Dwarves to protect them and, also for its safekeeping. Justice knew that in time the Devlins, as Drevilarche's followers came to be known, would survive on Goth Malin." She stopped her tale abruptly, "You must go to bed and rest!"

Jes was keen to ask more but with a dismissive and effective wave of her hand they found themselves in their individual bedchambers, luxurious and ornate.

It was frustrating to have so many unanswered questions, even Jasper and Jish who were knowledgeable about their own Lore had wanted to enquire further about the Dragon Lore. Each of them lay alone, thoughts whirring, but they nodded off simultaneously at a remote wave of Rhianne's hand from the Great Hall.

She continued gazing into the fire alongside Loro, Torro and Renewil, deep into the dark of the nel as the embers faded. She knew she had stated enough for them to complete their awesome task but was conscious of the danger facing each of the Chosen Ones, especially Emeriel.

Next pel, the travellers awoke alert and refreshed and initially the anxieties of the previous pel were gone. After eating the welcome snack thoughtfully left in each bedchamber, they found themselves transported onto the parapet, with Loro listening intently to Rhianne as she whispered into his large pointed ear.

When she had finished, she came across to Jes and in his hearing only she said, "You have been given the Mark of Justice. I know! It is of great importance on your forthcoming journey and in our future. You must use it wisely." She silenced him with a penetrating look. How could she know? He wondered in amazement.

She glanced up at the group, indicating they should embark. She waved solemnly, no smile to send them on their way to the Ferry of Goth Aref and their uncertain future. But had they turned back they would have seen the tears of sorrow in her troubled, sea-blue eyes as they departed. She wept inconsolably.

Loro flew valiantly into an uncertain future. Each of them was engulfed in a multitude of unanswered questions. Jes quietly mulled over Rhianne's words. He began to realise there was a connection between the scar, now the Mark, but how was he to use it wisely?

Unopened packs remained with illegible writing, and, it was hard for them not to speculate about the way ahead. The journey was short though and there was little time for reflection as they found themselves cruising to land at the Ferry. Confused, weary and apprehensive, they were not in the least prepared, for the devastating sight they were about to witness.

Chapter Eighteen

The Wrath of the Devlins

"How dare you!" She thought angrily as they walked invisibly, first, through the door and then, through Bigeviledd. She felt decidedly queasy passing through the disgusting odorous Devlin. On they went, melting into the far wall at the end of the corridor and then imperceptibly descending the stone stairs.

They were silently delighted to be leaving the dumbfounded Bigeviledd staring blankly at the vacant cells trying to figure out how to avoid Lord Madded's wrath. Their pleasure was short-lived. They reached the end of the third flight, and discovered a wall with a door inexplicably impenetrable to them even with their Giffts. Their mutual thought congratulations turned to intense irritation as they simultaneously walked into the wall, invisibly perhaps but still painfully, with a heavy, wounding thud.

"Now what?" Emeriel queried. The pain of the unexpected encounter whistled through her clenched teeth.

"Don't ask me?" Anuthel replied ruefully, rubbing his bruised head. He hopped around on one foot, nursing a stubbed toe. Despite everything Emeriel, being in the same dimension, couldn't help thinking how funny he looked.

"Alright that'll do…I don't understand this." He pondered pensively, "The Devlins barely have a workin' brain between them and yet our Giffts don't operate here. There must be an invisible barrier, but constructed by whom?"

Emeriel suddenly thought about the face she had seen before, the dark, daunting power behind Lord Madded. But determined to overcome whatever evil it may be, she blocked the thought from Anuthel and interjected, "Well, we'll just have to wait until they open the door!"

"That uses up our reserves. Body cloakin' costs internal energy and unless you have some spare Crillis or Emerene on your personage we've no means of replacin' it. We're gonna need it later that's fur sure." He shivered as he spoke.

She shook her head. But it left them little option except to sit and wait in the dark gloomy passage between the cold, uncomfortable steps and the door onto the courtyard.

"We should save our energy and de-cloak, shouldn't we then?" Emeriel suggested simply.

"Yes. But, we'll need to be alert, or we'll end up locked into a cell with walls like this one forever. Even the Devlins will tumble to that second time around if we get caught here." He inclined his head in the direction of the obstruction.

They waited apprehensively, but the only sound they heard was the continual oppressive thudding from below and voracious scratching from the usual occupants of the unending corridors of Goth Devlin.

"What is it?" Emeriel asked eventually. "That booming!"

"To be truthful, I'm not sure. It's one of the reasons I'm here. Deep in the Dwarf Mynes of Nilhunder, it is possible in the deepest myne to hear that very same sound. It was only noticed recently about 100 yers ago and Nodrogel, our leader, sent me from the Dwarf Council to find out what was going on. He suspected Devlin mischief.

"I explored the land between Nilhspring and the Straight of Goth Aref but could find nothin', even in the deepest ancient tunnels around Subterranium, but I noticed it got louder as I progressed Nilhward. I reported back to Nodrogel and he sent me on this mission to Goth Malin. Never did like me much!"

"Why do you say that?"

"Well it's not the sort of job you give to a friend, which is what I thought we were 20 yers ago, befur' he sent me."

"Maybe you were the only one he could trust!" She suggested.

"Well, that remains to be seen. Don't forget I've been waitin' a long time fur you in this awful place. He'll have forgotten about me." He said dejectedly, his voice tailing off

"Why didn't you use your Giffts to get yourself out before?"

"The Lore Book of Dwarves is very strict about use of Giffts. It was permitted that I could use them to help you as a Chosen One but not fur my own gain."

"Well, I'm not sure I would have been so patient."

"Justice would have banished me. I would have been replaced and I couldn't have finished my task which is considered an honour, though I have been gettin' grumpy about it the last 4 yers."

"4 yers!!!…"

"Yes, but don't forget, time passes differently when you're immortal. And anyway," He went on bravely, "I knew you were comin'." He added. "Although you are one of the Chosen Ones, many of your thoughts seem very different from what I expected."

Emeriel began to thought block rapidly, to avoid him knowing just how human, homesick and lonely she was feeling. She hadn't had any Crillis for some while and was feeling quite unlike a Chosen One.

Anuthel sympathetically sensed her need for quiet thinking time. They sat quietly for what turned into the rest of the pel and much of the nel. Weary and low, they fell into a deep, exhausted sleep until the early pel, not that they had any way of measuring time other than by the degree of their hunger.

When the latch on the heavy door suddenly clunked it jolted them out of their reverie, they hastily body cloaked simultaneously. Brendded lumbered clumsily and loudly into the corridor, and without delay they took their chance, nipping out into the empty courtyard before the door closed again.

"Shall we make our way to the surface?"

"It is so many yers since I was here. But unless somethin' has changed there is no way off the cliff. Is there? There are passages which lead elsewhere on this Justice-forsaken Island and also one which runs under the Straight of Goth Aref accordin' to the Ancient Lore 'though how we'll ever find it…" He broke off, hopelessly lost.

"Well we must try!" Emeriel's reply was firm and determined. "But not before we have unravelled the mysterious noise. Won't Nodrogel expect you to find out before you return?" She gently chided him encouragingly.

"Yyeess! But he's also gonna expect me to keep you safe. These two plans might not coincide. The thuddin' sounds dangerous and if you suffer I'll not be popular in Nilhspring or anywhere else on Faerspring, come to that!"

"Then, we'll have to find out what the noise is and escape safely. Won't we?" She used a tone instantly recognisable to both Jes and Jenna as one with which you don't disagree, except they weren't there, and, unfortunately, it was lost on Anuthel, who continued to thought argue as they picked a careful passage across the courtyard.

They were still in dispute, as they sped down the steps, reaching the first fork in the tunnels. Emeriel remembered being there with Brendded but had been so frightened then she could not recall which way led back to the Fortress, so their quarrel became irrelevant and Anuthel's adamant, "I have to get you to safety!" was neither here nor there. He did not know which way 'safety' was!

However, being a Dwarf and being used to caverns and tunnels, he felt confident, despite his lack of knowledge, deciding on the tunnel branching to the right and sloping upwards. Emeriel followed knowing he thought this would lead them away from the ominous sound but she put a thought block on her nagging suspicion that this was not the case. Each junction he chose, despite his best Dwarf intuition, the Chosen One suspected they were getting closer to her own goal of finding the source of the sound. She followed, meek as a lamb, until he sighed audibly.

"We're getting nearer to whatever it is and I'm doing my best to avoid it. My mother always said I had a useless sense of direction!"

Emeriel responded, "Well I'm sure we're meant to find out, maybe it's part of what I'm meant to do here?"

"You may be right but I can't say I'm happy 'bout it. I'm supposed to protect you from evil and the louder that noise becomes the more certain I am it's very evil…"

"..And, therefore, we should actively seek it out and destroy it!" She finished firmly. They came to another crossroads. This time there were two obvious choices, either downwards or up along one of three tunnels.

They looked at each other, no going back this time? "Down we go then, Emeriel. Are you sure?" Anuthel's eyes held a concerned, earnest look, not the usual laughing glint.

"Yes. Let's go!" Emeriel led the way into the twisting, turning tunnels, partly unlit and with steps at unpredictable intervals. At each descending step, the noise volume intensified and, on a background of unwelcome scurrying sounds, they could feel an increasing shuddering running through their weary bodies. There were no further junctions and they wound their way even deeper for two Faermills or more.

Emeriel imposed a thought block during this time as she was becoming afraid, uneasy about what they might ultimately face, knowing that if Anuthel became aware of it he would regret their decision, turn around and head for safety. He had also constructed a thought block, for similar reasons, though they were both so preoccupied with the other's welfare, neither noticed. When they came to a large bright cavern they were startled out of their personal brooding with a jolt.

It was so well lit it was unnerving but by body cloaking immediately they had opportunity to survey the cavern carefully. It had a high vaulted ceiling with stalactites reaching menacingly down toward them and figure-like stalagmites at the periphery of their vision.

The walls glistened with running water, light reflecting from numerous flickering torches and there were wooden barrels stacked neatly, marked with the sign of a blood red skull, a Devlin-shaped skull, of course. 'Ink', hopefully, Emeriel thought. There were hundreds of them. She was about to ask Anuthel what he thought they were when she suddenly became aware of a moving stalagmite. As she neared it she realised it was in fact a dozing Devlin. She nudged Anuthel gently to alert him and he nodded, acknowledging her warning.

They moved silently, traversing the cavern into another tunnel, where by stark contrast, light was absent and they had to feel their way cautiously along the walls. They could hear a gentle trickling in the distance. "Stream maybe?" Emeriel wondered, as she felt the wall on the right disappear without warning. Instinctively, she moved closer to the remaining wall on the left.

"Yes. I sensed water underground back in the cavern and we have descended even further since." Anuthel responded sounding knowledgeable.

"How did you know? I couldn't hear it!"

"I am a Dwarf, Emeriel. I live much of my life in tunnels and caves. It is part of my nature to source underground water. Now concentrate as I fear this gully may be very deep and some way below even though it sounds so near."

Too late! Her foot slipped on a loose rock and she plunged headlong over the edge, desperately outstretching her arms to reach and grab on to something, anything! She clung like a limpet for all she was worth to what turned out to be Anuthel's ankle and a jutting rock edge. For a few moments, she was steady, and then the rocks crumbled away. She found herself hanging precariously in thin air by one hand, swinging the other frantically.

"Help!" She panicked as she tried to suppress an audible scream of terror.

"Hold on!" Anuthel struggled to haul her back over the edge. He ignored her, "What else am I going to do? Hurry up!"

"We can't go on like this! We need some light and unless you have a special Gifftin' in that area we'll have to go back and borrow a torch."

She agreed wholeheartedly, with his sentiments, and, rising shakily to her feet, he caught, "For sure!"

Carefully turning around they clung tenaciously to the wall and slowly retraced their steps to the cavern, only to find the previously dozing Devlin wide-awake and grunting to himself miserably. He was moving barrels into the centre, adjacent to a hitherto unseen, open trapdoor and slowly lowering them down through the trapdoor on a rope. One by one, he let them down, grumbling all the while, until he had finished. Then he slammed the door shut, threw a filthy rug over it and collapsed clumsily onto it.

"No wonder we didn't spot it before!" Emeriel was relieved they had not missed it through lack of observation. Anuthel felt similarly and was anxious to avoid overlooking anything else that might be important.

"D'you think we should explore a bit more before we grab the torch? I'm wonderin' how these barrels got here. We can see how they're leavin'…" and as if to emphasise his point there was an unexpected loud rolling sound, as a barrel careered into view, apparently from nowhere.

As they shifted to get a better vantage point, another fell hitting a large stalagmite on their left. It soon became clear that there was a barrel-size chute hollowed out from the cavern wall. Barrel after barrel arrived with crash after thudding crash. After twenty or so had tumbled in, there was a heavy thump as another trapdoor banged shut. This woke the lazy Devlin out of his snooze; further dark muttering ensued as he lumbered to his feet to begin shifting the barrels again.

"That answers that!" Emeriel quipped. "Let's grab the torch and get out of here."

"I'm with you on that" replied Anuthel as he blew out the nearest torch on the wall.

As the Devlin grudgingly heaved the heavy barrels, he was too busy muttering, "Barrels…Madded…Food," to notice that one torch had gone out.

Anuthel seized his chance and snatched the smoking torch incorporating it within his body cloak. He and Emeriel then hurriedly made their way back into the tunnel pausing briefly to relight the torch as they dashed out of the cavern. Had the grumbling Devlin been looking, he would have been very puzzled to see the sudden glowing light with no obvious source, body cloaking concealing the torch and flame, but not the light emanating from it.

They were soon passing the precipice over which Emeriel had fallen. She shuddered when she saw the stream now clearly visible in the gully, many Faermatres below. Bravely thought blocking, she shrugged and bypassed the ledge but Anuthel knew how perilously close to death she had been and how afraid she felt. He closed the distance between them, giving her a reassuring Dwarfish thump across the shoulders, catching her by surprise.

They both smiled fleetingly and trudged on in silence winding their way along the rocky edge carefully. The stream below gradually meandered its way into a river, with so many twists and turns they had not realised they were almost directly below the bright cavern until they saw more barrels springing into view ahead.

Anuthel extinguished the torch hurriedly, as they studied the scene. The river ran along the edge of the cavern floor. It was a vast space and scores of Devlins worked busily.

"Still slow and clumsy, but I've never seen so many, so active!" Anuthel chuckled at Emeriel's thought.

Some were heaving the dropped barrels and stacking them by the river. Others loaded barrels onto wooden jetties, positioned at intervals along the riverbank, flat-bottomed boats moored alongside. Each boat was already packed with four or five barrels and looked overloaded, at that. Several Devlins were lying around either sleeping or complaining but the supervisor, stockier and with darker features than the others, shouted at them angrily.

"No slackers here!" Anuthel was peering upwards, "Look that's the trapdoor, we saw before."

"There's so many of them!"

"Yeah and there's obviously some hurry about all this. Never seen 'em move so fast or taking so few meal breaks." Anuthel added.

Their mind discussion was interrupted by an unexpected roaring noise from the far end of the cavern. A huge gaping hole appeared as an enormous rock slid to one side allowing the thudding to suddenly become clearer, ear shattering. Try as they might they were not able to see what lay beyond, other than darkness and a dull, crimson glow in the distant gloom. Then the hole was gone. Neither of them could figure out reason for the opening but were relieved at the relative peace when it closed.

They continued to observe boats arriving, barrels being stowed and then departing down the river. Emeriel stifled bubbling laughter as one dim looking Devlin piled one barrel too many onto the boat nearest to them. It capsized in glorious slow motion into the water, soaking himself to the momentary amusement of his fellow workers. This caused further noisy abuse from the supervisor.

"I've never seen them laugh before, have you?"

"There in't much fur 'em to laugh about and they in't usually quick enuff to git the joke either. But mebbe thir' so busy they're lettin' off steam a bit. Now how do we get outta 'ere?" Anuthel's Dwarf dialect was accentuated by his anxiety to be on the way.

Emeriel fixed him with a steady gaze, "On one of those." She glanced across at the upended boat and the continuing antics of the drenched Devlin, frantically waving his arms in an attempt to get some help. "We hide on one and make our way downstream with the barrels. Find out where they're headed and what the noise is."

Anuthel looked disconcerted, "Now…. That's not a good idea…I don't swim… Dwarves don't, nor Devlins as you can see. We have the same ancestry."

He was still objecting as Emeriel passed by him before he could stop her. She smiled sweetly at him. Body cloaked she left the safety of the tunnel for the bright light of the cavern, carefully avoiding Devlins as she went. Anuthel acquiesced, following her reluctantly, he was beginning to recognise that determined look and knew the pointlessness of starting a dispute. He, too, was being vigilant, trying not to collide with any clumsy Devlin but with his bulky frame he found it much more difficult than Emeriel. So inevitably, though they were almost at the riverbank, he bumped into the half-drowned Devlin, now trying to reload his boat. In the ensuing commotion Anuthel and Emeriel were able to scramble aboard another boat that was ready to leave.

Anuthel was worried by the comments he could hear as they passed though, "It 'it me I tell you!" The wet Devlin was insistent. He had fallen in again, as a result of his barging encounter with Anuthel, sending the barrels flying once more.

Fortunately the Supervisor was having none of it, "That's it you. Down to the Hall of Wrath for the rest of the shift!"

"Noooo! Noooo! It wasn't me! It was that... that...whatever 'it me." Despite his protests, however, two suitably armed guards took away the misunderstood, bedraggled Devlin. Meanwhile, Emeriel adjusted her position behind a barrel at the stern, causing a lurching of the overloaded craft. "Stop that! I can't swim."

Anuthel's tone held a note of panic. As a Devlin loosed a rope at the aft they moved off slowly downstream. He used a single oar to propel the boat, extremely precariously, as Emeriel could see from her perspective. Anuthel could not see, which was just as well.

The river was flowing faster now and they meandered along in the darkness. The oarsmen had stopped rowing and was only steering, as the current swept them onwards. The thudding intensified at each turn of the river. Reflecting in the murky darkness, they wondered how it all fitted together.

That was when Anuthel first noticed the faint, sickly odour leaking from the barrels, thick, fishy and nauseating. He knew he was going to retch. Emeriel understanding his predicament knew, that once he started heaving, it would be audible to the Devlin. Body cloaking had serious limitations and inability to obscure sound was one of them. It was not long before her fears were confirmed and the Devlin was alerted to their presence. Thinking fast, she blew out the torch at the helm, catapulting them into darkness. This confused the Devlin, not difficult, even in normal circumstances.

She crept toward him, along the narrow edge, past the barrels and gave him a shove so he fell onto the flat deck and then whilst he was still reeling with the shock, she jumped on him. Anuthel had managed to get a grip on his nausea by this point, and, hastily made his way to aid her.

They quickly had the advantage of the powerful but stupid, startled Devlin, and binding his hands and feet with their belts they sat back, relieved until the boat scraping along the channel wall reminded them that they were now unguided. Thankfully, the oar was still in its lock. Emeriel grabbed it, and remembering the way the Devlin had steered, managed to regain control, navigating the boat back into the current.

"Ok! What now?"

Chapter Nineteen

Nelida

An enormous, fierce fireball exploded above the Island of Goth Malin and the mammoth shock waves reverberated below and far beyond them. Even in distant Ilvwood, they felt the shuddering impact. A dark cloud mushroomed on the horizon, smoke and ashes rained down across Faerspring.

"What the Justice was that?" Jish swore, uncharacteristically. A rosy pink glow developed, instead of the usual green, as the low suns light shone hazily through the thick smoke and ash, that peleve. It reminded Jes of a far away place he knew as, home…

A further eruption of glittering colours from the Faerspring spectrum of light, followed. Jes and Jenna had never seen the like; some were darker than black and others were indescribable to them with a luminous quality. Jes glanced down at the Mark and was not surprised to see the black pulsation once more. It chilled him and he gasped.

Jish and Jasper gasped too, "Iridichium…. Rosper…. Clospel!!!" They could feel as well as see the colours. It was eerie. The sky shimmered with a crimson haze and the sea turned deep blood red.

Loro flew deftly downwards, through the hail of debris. The high wood fencing encompassing the garrison of Ferry Mollin became more easily discernible through the gloom. It looked inviting in the rosy glow but as they neared it, the chaos below grew evident. Ilves, Faerspringians, Dwarves and other races, they had not previously encountered, could be seen dashing around in a dazed state and, of course, the arrival of the Lorduress, just, added to the confusion.

As they landed amidst the turmoil, Jes shouted to Jasper, "Where's Jeruthel?"

Jasper attempted to control the uproar. He grabbed the next passer-by who happened to be a purple skinned Ilf-like creature, "Bring me Jeruthel, immediately! He is expecting us." He commanded loudly and abruptly, Rhianne would have been proud of him; as would Twit, but not for his sharp manner, rather for his confidence! This spontaneously created an unexpected hush in the complex, milling crowd, in spite of the ongoing fireworks on high. Only an occasional, distracted, backward glance of curiosity, from the audience, testified to the persisting atmospheric display. Jenna was still bemused and knew she would never see such a sight again.

There were gasps from the assembled group, "Lorduress!" "It is time." This is it!" "They are here!" Loro rose admirably to the occasion, puffing his chest with pride and almost unsaddling them. The reaction was disarming but they tried to live up to the high expectations of their admirers, disembarking with all the grace and elegance they could muster.

In a flash, the dark hooded figure of Jeruthel was before them. The hoards melted away and they found themselves alone with an intimidating being.

"I am here." His voice was thick and full of foreboding. They were all determined to be bold and confident, in view of his previous suggestions, nevertheless Torro, trembling uncontrollably behind Jenna's calves, was an external indicator of the group's most intimate feelings.

"Pleased to meet you," Jes replied, sternly, "We have the Key from Princess Rhianne, so if you would be so kind as to show us the Ferry, we'll not trouble you further."

"Nooo!" roared Jeruthel. "You cannot cross in this storm. You will perish within moments. You will achieve nothing." And as the brave, but unobservant, group looked across the Straight of Goth Aref they realised it was not only the sky in turmoil but the sea also.

There were vast, white, crested waves pounding the shore and although the Straight was narrow, common sense dictated they could not reach the other side, barely visible through the storm and smoke. The sea was boiling and frothing like a cauldron, even Jes could see the dark strangers' viewpoint.

"Maybe it will settle down." Jenna suggested, politely and somewhat hopefully.

"Not tonel!" Jeruthel insisted. "Please follow me." A surly gruffness belied evident hospitality. He led them to a low thatched barn-like building.

As the doors swung back the warmth embraced them, pervading their cold, exhausted bodies. They began to relax.

The heterogeneous company, sitting around circular wooden tables playing various board games, chatting, drinking Gripple Juice from tankards and eating, composed a peculiar scene. There were a host of dialects and tongues in use. There were many animated discussions regarding the explosion and debates about the possible source. Jeruthel invited them to be seated and a strange one-eyed creature with a bluish-hue skin brought refreshments.

He introduced himself, "Yilid, pleased to be of service." He slapped his right hand across his left shoulder.

Jeruthel explained this was the customary greeting from a Yed, from the distant land of Yedr to the far Elh beyond Nilhspring. He told them that though Yeds were Ilf-like in appearance, quietly spoken and thoughtful like their ancient cousins, they differed in that they lived off the sea and seashore, rather than the forest.

It was hard for the travellers, not to stare rudely around the room, at so many unusual creatures. Fortunately, Jeruthel understood their curiosity, and seemed happy to explain. Jes thought he wasn't so bad after all as he introduced them to the strangest looking group of all, the Moralusians. They were tiny creatures, smaller even than the shortest of the Dwarves, Faerie-like in stature but with a lengthy tail and flaring nostrils on a snout with fangs. They spoke in Faerspringian dialect though and had Faerspringian eyes.

Torro spent the nel, under the Moralusian table; clearing up dropped food and instinctively seemed to know he shared his ancestry with them. The Moralusians dropped him titbits and he allowed them to fuss him.

Jeruthel instructed Yilid to ensure the Dwarf cook for the garrison brought out some Crillis and Emerene for his weary guests. The crowd were friendly and hospitable, regaling them with stories from Lore Books of their races. They learned that the Moralusians originated from a peninsula to the Far Welh of Nilhspring. Moriell was the town from which this particular group hailed. They told of the time when Justice had banished Drevilarche to the Nether World and how his scattered minions had gradually slimed back regrouping and hiding in Goth Malin.

Since that time, Justice had bestowed upon them the task of keeping the waters of Faerspring pure, to ensure the Devlins could not poison the springs and wipe out the other inhabitant

Some of the tales, they heard that nel, were in song, dedicated to the honour of individual heroes. One song told of a brave Moralusian, called Morna, and lived long after in their memories. It told of her battle with Drevilarche himself, when he was attempting to poison the Nilhspring.

"One fine pel, way back in time,

Brave Morna lived, in the town of Thime,

She was bold and true of heart and mind,

She bent arrows flight, to make them wind....

Sung with feeling by Lorolye, as the rendition finished, there were many tear-filled eyes. It was late. Exhausted by their concerns of the explosion and it's meaning, many prepared to bed down, for the nel. Jeruthel had been kind to the Chosen Ones and when he had relaxed sufficiently, letting his hood down, they were conscious at last of his kindly face. His stern voice replaced by a helpful flow of advicc and information.

He told them of the Devlin weaknesses, poor eyesight in the suns and poor communication skills. He warned them of their strengths, thick hides and aggression. Most importantly he told them that any wound in the hidden eye was fatal to a Devlin and would cause them to be condemned forever to the Nether World.

Eventually he showed the drained group to a nearby thatched hut, poosy feather mattresses were laid out on rush mats, covering the stone floor. The fire in the fireplace blazed away merrily in the middle of the floor and a central metal chimney funnelled the wood smoke out into the valley.

A Dwarf, who had been assigned to take care of them, brought thick fur rugs. Since the Nilh had such a cold climate, they were glad of them as they snuggled down that nel.

Renewil and Torro were absent. Renewil had found another owline amongst the numerous creatures at the Ferry village and was still out and about with his newfound friend. Torro had become so attached to the Moralusians and one, called Moriani, in particular. He had followed her back to her bed where he was now cosily snuggled down at her feet, tails intertwined, as though he had been her lifelong pet. Jenna missed him but sensed that he belonged with his new friends.

They were all asleep instantly, except Jes who lay awake trying to fit the pieces of this frightening and confusing puzzle together. He had to find and rescue Emeriel. He feared the explosion had involved her. He turned events over and over, in his mind. Why had Ariella had tears in her eyes when she read the Lore Book? Why did so many of those they had encountered refuse to tell them what they obviously knew? He felt the meeting with the Moralusians held special significance but had no idea what.

The clouds of confusion drifted into clouds of sleep and he began to dream about hundreds of flying Lorduress' under attack from flaming missiles fired from huge Devlin catapults. One was saddled, closely guarded and protected, by others nearby.

Many were wounded and were falling to the ground. Their desperate efforts were in vain though and Jes felt so helpless as he watched this special Lorduress carrying four regal-looking passengers being hit and falling into the sea. His concern intensified as he noticed two of them were children. Jes was shouting, "No! No!" as he woke up with a start.

He lay awake once more, tossing and turning, thinking about what he had seen and then, finally drifted back into a deep, dreamless sleep, like the others.

At early pellight, the friendly Dwarf, Mathuel, bustled in, "Good pel to ye! Did ye sleep well?" He chuckled. "How about a bit of pelfirst?" He didn't need to ask twice, they had all awakened starving and, dressing quickly, followed him across the yard to the Gathering Hut. Renewil, Torro and several of their sleepy headed companions from the nel before, were already tucking into a hearty pelfirst. It was traditional Nilhern fare consisting of an oat mixture, thick and full of goodness, mixed with cream from the local Colly Herd. They sat down. There was little conversation and everyone seemed in a reflective mood.

Jeruthel arrived, greeting them courteously, "Goodpel, my friends. I trust you slept well and that Mathuel took good care of you." He slapped the helpful Dwarf on the back. "We must make ready for their crossing, before the storm rises again. Prepare the supplies."

They finished quickly and followed Jeruthel to the Ferryside. It was near the stable where Loro had been resting over nel. They had not seen him since their arrival and were relieved to find he had been well nourished and cared for. It was then that Jenna suddenly realised Loro would not be continuing with them.

"He is coming with us isn't he?" Jenna whispered to Jes. Loro heard and shook his head sadly. "Why not?" Jenna directed the question loudly to Loro, not caring now whether Jeruthel heard or not. He snorted a few puffs of smoke as she stroked him and, before he could respond, Jeruthel interrupted.

"He cannot Jenna. He has another task to accomplish here. You will not need him in your onward journey. Please bid him, 'Goodbye'."

Jes gave her a look, which she knew, meant, "Don't argue" and sadly, with heavy hearts, they said "Farewell" to Loro. He had been vital to their journey and Jes wondered whether there was a connection between his half-remembered dream and leaving Loro, but if so he could not grasp the elusive thread.

The Ferry was moored at the small quay, a grand title for what was little more than a rowing boat with a flimsy sail.

"The Key, please?" They looked around at each other.

Renewil was late, but turned up moments later, clumsily careering into Jeruthel accompanied by his new friend. Jeruthel looked cross. Renewil hastily passed Jeruthel the Key and he unlocked a tiny padlock holding the Ferry rope to the mooring.

Amazingly simple really, until Jeruthel spoke, "You must take care friends. This Ferry was last used to collect an Ancient Herbal Healing remedy from Aref's Head for a wound of Princess Rhianne's, several Faer centuries ago."

"That's reassuring," said Jes, with heavy sarcasm. "So we know its sea worthy then!"

"Don't worry, my friend, it has been kept in good order ready for this very day. Remember we have been expecting you."

He beckoned the crew to board the tiny vessel, as they embarked it took on an eerie glow and the mist gathering on the sea engulfed the boat. Loro, Torro and Renewil remained on the quay waving, downcast. Jeruthel stood with them, "I wish you well." He whispered, pushing the boat from it's mooring

"Aren't you coming?" Jish enquired anxiously. Jenna realised that Jish was about to be seasick.

"No, Jish, that is not my role. You will not need me. I am required here." He replied ceremoniously as the distance increased between them. "I wish you success in your onward journey. May Justice be with you!"

The ferry drifted silently into the mist, and before they could reply Jeruthel was gone. The Ferry seemed to propel itself, but when they turned to see what lay ahead they were startled to see a mysterious hooded figure in white flowing robes standing in the prow, one hand held out and with a gnarled pointing finger, which seemed to part the swirling mist.

The wary group looked at each other in stunned silence, fear haunting their eyes. Jes checked the Mark and noted its pale blue tint, he felt reassured but only a little! The figure turned to face them. Alarmed, they realised the hood protected no head, there was only a horrifying darkness where a face should have been. A sinister guffaw of cackling laughter erupted from within. The hood fell off to reveal a diminutive wizened old Faerie with white flowing locks and wrinkled skin.

Their fear evaporated instantly, as she said mischievously, "Did you enjoy the show? Good aren't I? Mind you, I've practised for many a yer."

"Why?" Jes was irritated at having been made to feel so heart-stoppingly afraid unnecessarily.

"Well, I've had some pretty weird and evil passengers in my time, so I like to keep mystery and atmosphere on my side. In your case, I knew an exception would be best; you may need my help on the return journey and I thought you should know I could be trusted."

"Hold on!" Jes interrupted suspiciously, "We appreciate your honesty but that proves nothing. I guess Jeruthel entrusted us to your care…."

"Wait." It was Jaspers turn to interject, "She wasn't here when we embarked, remember."

The Faerie tilted her head to one side, eyeing them with curiosity, "You don't trust me? Though aside from Jeruthel, I've never revealed myself to travellers before…Aah well, you'll have to make up your own minds. You're going nowhere without me."

She sat down next to Jish, folded her arms with great deliberation and turned around to stare into the mist as the Ferry drifted aimlessly.

Jes could see her point and decided, whether or not she was trustworthy; they would remain adrift on the Straight of Goth Aref forever, without her. He had also deduced that Jeruthel had been adamant he was not needed, which implied he knew they would be fine without him. But what if Jeruthel….

His thoughts were interrupted by an unexpected parting of the mist, which revealed another explosive display of light accompanied by the same thunderous noise as the previous peleve. He checked the Mark although he knew already. "Devlins!"

The old Faerie murmured, confirming Jes' intuition and the black pulsation Jes had glimpsed, "They've been at it for two pel now. They're up to no good." She shook her head as she went on, "There's been strange happenings for several flers. First, there have been more of them about. Then there's been shipments of Caltimile rock and hundreds of barrels. I spoke about it with my mistress and she told me to continue watching." She looked back toward the fiery red lights, "Now this! You still want me to carry on over so you can find your friend?"

They nodded numbly trying to understand the sight before them, wondering whether Emeriel could possibly be alive amidst the chaos.

Meanwhile, Nelida, as they had discovered she was called, looked anxious, "Black Drakes!" she explained these were Devlin created storms and very bad news. Sadly, the evidence had started to engulf them, already purple-black, nebulous fog enveloped them and the waves began to deepen, rocking their craft violently. The evil was palpable in the very air. The Mark confirmed it.

"Do not fear. I can help you." She began waving her arms at the worsening storm, "Justice, I seek your help. Mistress, of the Lesser Path of the Sea Wevil, aid us." Despite her efforts, the foaming crests on the mountainous waves were all too obvious.

"How much further?" Jish asked heaving over the side of the flimsy Balsaid boat, made from the light, buoyant wood of the Limebrack tree. Jenna rummaged through the knapsack and discovered 'Sea-sick remedy', and Jish was very grateful.

Nelida was busy battling with the evil surrounding them, flashes of blue light emanating from her tiny figure. That was when Dariatha, the Devlin Demon of the Sea made an overwhelming appearance. His craggy black leathery head pushed up through the water, four times the size of the boat, causing a tidal wave to sweep furiously toward them. As soon as Nelida espied him she locked him somehow in a shaft of white light, which she called down from above.

Paralysed by her, he floated helplessly until she struck with mighty force. The demon disappeared below, causing another great wave that sent the Ferry, Nelida and the stunned crew into watery oblivion. When Dariatha reappeared Nelida was ready for him, transfiguring dramatically to the crest of an enormous wave she incanted furiously and threw a tremendous bolt of blue light at him. The outer layers of his flesh dissolved into a luminous green gel, causing him to vanish, finally. The boiling sea calmed instantly, the purple black mist evaporated to reveal the crew and the upturned Ferry.

Jes reached out to rescue Jenna, just as she was sinking beneath the surface gasping and choking. Jasper looked in vain for Jish. Nelida joined him in his search. Somehow Jes managed to right the boat and helped Jenna into it with a great deal of effort.

Nelida maintained her stance above the water with apparent ease and miraculously was not even damp but, even with her Giffts, she was unable to see or hear Jish. Jes scrambled carefully across to try and help Jasper.

They called frantically for Jish but it was hopeless, Jenna sobbed inconsolably.

"We must go on. There is danger here. Jish would not want us to linger and jeopardise the mission or put your lives at risk further." Nelida, now back in the boat with them, spoke sadly but firmly. So they continued on sombrely.

Jes hugged Jenna whilst Jasper stared silently into the gloom. With his in-depth knowledge of the Lore he knew the words of comfort but he felt comfortless and there was no explanation in the Lore for what had happened to Jish. They were immortal so where was he? He could not be in the Nether World. He belonged to Justice. But he was gone and Jasper had never faced such an incident before. He had known Jish since they both arrived at the Timewatchers Tower many Faercenturies ago.

"Where is he Nelida? I know he cannot be dead but where is he?" He hoped this wise old Faerie would give him some words of consolation.

Nelida looked piercingly into his eyes, replying, "Tell me what you think Jasper, you know the Lore well!"

"He is gone! The Lore states that only the evil go the Nether World. But both Methven and Jish are gone. Are they in the Place Beyond? But, what if the Devlins have succeeded in reversing the natural order…." He fumbled for words, afraid of hearing the truth. " None have died since before the Great Death so….

"You are all in grave danger, Jasper, and are on Devlin territory. Remember their Laws govern this wicked place in which you are travelling. They have reversed the natural laws of Justice here, I have heard of deaths in this land and know they are seeking to pervert Faerspring with their evil order. I do not know where your friends are, but I do know you must not give in now."

Nelida turned away to hide the tears coursing down her age worn face. She knew not where their friends were, but could guess and if she shared her suspicion she feared they would be unable to complete their challenge, resulting in many more unnecessary deaths. So she continued incanting, parting the mist as they glided on.

The skies were darkening again and storm clouds gathered with flashes of red lightening. Rain fell in sheets and the waves were fierce. Chilled and soaked to the bone, they were desolate and overwhelmed with sorrow. The knapsack had been lost overboard.

Jes could visualise its location in his mind. He focused, fighting against his emotions, and concentrating intently, he employed his Gifft. It took a supreme effort but after a while he could see it floating at the side of the boat. He reached out and hauled it, sodden out of the water. With typical Ilvish Providence, it dried immediately.

The Ferry was slowly filling with water and Nelida instructed them to bail it out with whatever they could find, as fast as they could, while she devoted her energies to fend off the storm and the increasing powers of Goth Malin.

Jes rifled through the knapsack and to no one's surprise his hand alighted on a package labelled, 'Bailing Out' and another, 'Drying Out'. He opened and employed the former. Jenna roused herself from her grief to use the latter to comfort and dry Jasper. The Ilvish towel worked wonderfully for drying skin but not for drying tears and still Jasper remained bereft, comfortless in his grief. Time passed slowly.

Eventually, they could see high dark cliffs towering up piercing the leaden mists; pillars of sheer faced rock with no crevices or footholds. Jes looked carefully for some way to climb up. Fiery flashes of light flared at the stark cliffs intermittently, providing sufficient light to confirm there would be no ascent that way.

Nelida turned and reassuringly mouthed, "Don't worry, I know a route in."

It was only then that Jes realised she had the same thought knowledge Gifft they had previously encountered. He was so busy thinking about the implications of this he scarcely noticed they had sailed right under the vast cliffs into a tunnel. Still propping up the sleeping Jenna, exhausted through sobbing, he turned to ask Nelida where they were but she was gone.

Continuing on in the darkness, the Ferry was under self-propulsion once more. Nelida's disappearance caused them to feel vulnerable and lonely in the void and the loss of Jish still lingered achingly in their hearts and minds.

Astonishingly and at close proximity, an enormous fireball rose out of nowhere, followed by a tidal wave, which sent them hurtling back out to sea. A cloud of ashes and smoke billowed several Faermills high into the already stormy sky, surely visible across the whole of Faerspring.

"What the Justice was that?" swore Jasper. A pink glow enveloped everything in sight. There were several further explosions. "Emeriel!" cried Jenna, now wide-awake. "What about Emeriel?"

Unexpectedly, out of the haze, Nelida reappeared in the bow. "That was quite something! I think that's put paid to them for a while." Jes continued to worry; Emeriel could not possibly be alive on the Island after that. Scanning the horizon with burning eyes, he realised that only a miracle could have saved her. Next to him, Jenna stifled her sobs.

Chapter Twenty

Emeriel's Discovery

The boat gently glided, in the inexperienced, but determined, hands of Emeriel. Anuthel continued his helpless retching and it was clear to Emeriel that he could go no further, apologetic though he was. She, too, was physically weak and knew she was ready to drop. It was then she noticed an opening in the rock wall and with steadily increasing skill, she guided the craft into it. Fortunately there was a shallow rock shelf and Emeriel beached the boat firmly, wedging the oar in to prevent any movement.

There, they collapsed. The safely restrained Devlin was sleeping, exhausted from his struggles. To be sure he would not escape Emeriel instructed Anuthel to lean on him from one side and she did the same from the other. They fell asleep in the darkness, despite the disgusting smelling Devlin. They awoke next pel, stiff and cold. Anuthel was famished to the point of death; Dwarves detesting hunger, tolerated it poorly and as Emeriel fast discovered, he was in an appalling mood. Grumbling at each other, they had great difficulty getting the boat off the shelf in order to recommence their journey. Emeriel quickly found the rhythm and it was not long before Anuthel began his retching again. He could not help himself though and although he had vowed during the long, dark nel to be brave, as soon as the rocking rolling motion began, he started up anew.

Emeriel tried to communicate her thoughts to him, but his mind was elsewhere, when she tried to alert him to the sight around the bend of the river, he was oblivious. There was a ghostly, vermilion shimmer over the water and revealed before them was yet another huge cavern. This one, though, was so enormous Emeriel could neither see the opposite side nor the ceiling. Fortunately, it was dimly lit and there was such activity they slipped unnoticed into a long stream of boats, joining them from several other passages.

"Anuthel!" Emeriel thought, with loud irritation, "What next?" She was still body cloaked, as was he, but she was certain it would not be long before even the dimmest, half asleep Devlin would figure there was something amiss with a boat rowing itself. In a flash of inspiration, and under pressure from her rising panic, she decided that the bound Devlin might provide an air of normality, if propped in an appropriate position.

"Anuthel, any chance you could help me prop up our friend, here, so we don't look quite so conspicuous? If not, maybe you employ one of your Giffts? Now, would be good!"

Anuthel shook his head, miserably, "Not feeling like this. Can't you just moor somewhere and we can mingle, while I recover. I'm sorry." And he vomited again, emphasising his point.

Before she had chance to respond, they became the centre of attention, watched by open-mouthed Devlins, crowding onto the riverbank and pointing at them.

"Great!"

"Oh dear! This is my fault!"

"Let's ditch our friend overboard. They'll have to rescue him and that might give us a chance to go over the side of the boat and make our way to the bank. What do you think?" Once again, Emeriel's quick thinking was getting them out of considerable danger.

"OK Let's do it!" Anuthel already felt he had let her down and, despite waves of nausea, he was determined not to do so again. Without further discussion, they tipped the wide-eyed, panic stricken Devlin into the freezing water with a loud and visible splash. The Devlin' workers' lack of enthusiasm for water, proved the burly, drowning Devlin to be the ideal decoy. Fighting broke out amongst them, bravery not one of their strong points, and none of them wanted to get wet rescuing him, preferring to fight until they could force a weaker Devlin into an act of heroism!

Emeriel glanced back as she scrambled over the side of the boat. She wondered whether they were so evil they might not even bother trying to save one of their own kind. Anuthel followed her, relieved to be getting off the sick-making boat at last. Emeriel swam, as gently and splash free as possible, toward the bank and heard Anuthel desperately sploshing along noisily behind her. She went back to help him and using survival techniques learned in a parallel world for a badge, she eventually dragged him to the bank. In the difficult process, she concluded that the reason Dwarves were so afraid of water was because they were not blessed with any buoyancy. He had disappeared beneath the surface in several anxious moments. Fortunately for Anuthel she had been a keen and enthusiastic pupil on earth.

Thankfully there was such a commotion on the opposite bank their noisy swim had gone unnoticed. One of the Devlin Sergeants had forced several Devlins into the water to fetch the wretched Boat Keeper; by the time they had finally rescued him, albeit half-dead, Anuthel and Emeriel were well away along the bank. The Devlin Supervisors had not even begun to consider the implications of the scene they had witnessed.

Emeriel saw a large, wooden vat, in the centre of the cavern, which funnelled into a cauldron, partially buried in the rock floor. Hundreds of skull-marked barrels were being emptied into the vat, by hoards of Devlins scrambling up wooden scaffolding. The substance being poured appeared to be a thick, pitch-black gel.

The booming noise from below was now deafening and Emeriel wondered about the significance of the vat and how everything related. Sporadically, the cauldron would empty, refilling drop by drop from above. Something was being filled below where the noise seemed to originate. But what?

Anuthel intruded into her deliberations, "Good! Let's go then. You've seen it now and I have an idea about what is going on here. I think we're done, and anyway, I'm not feeling too good." Anuthel was desperate to get her to safety.

"We're not done yet. We need to find out what's going on below." Emeriel was not going to be dissuaded and dragged away having got this far. She was still searching for clues and she noticed an area nearby where hundreds of Devlins seemed to be disappearing and reappearing. Ignoring Anuthel's pleas, she moved nearer and realised there was a tunnel leading down an exceedingly steep flight of steps hewn out of the rock.

"This way, Anuthel I think we're about to get our answers. Then we can go." She led the way as he muttered silently behind her. They cautiously made their way between hurrying Devlins.

"They don't smell good in large numbers." Even Emeriel felt queasy.

"You're right about that, but there's another foul odour apart from their awful stench. Mmmm… It reminds me of something… Strychnopurine. I've come across it once before, in the Temple of the Dwarf Ecurelian Order. The Dwarf Priests protect and worship the Strychnopurine because of its potent power against the Lammymuirs, Devlinish little creatures, who inhabit the Deep Durelian Mynes. They only allow a small ration each yer for the Dwarves and it has to be used sparingly. It is closely regulated, only the Priests of Ecurelian know how it is produced, and it makes no sense at all that there are so many Faergallons here! But I'm sure that's the smell. It's unforgettable!"

"Maybe the Devlins have captured one of the Priests or Followers and they have told them how to make it… But what do they need it for?" Her thought trailed off, as an all-engulfing sound erupted from the tunnel they had been traversing.

"Employ your body cloak, to exclude the sound, concentrate hard and you will be able to block it out."

Emeriel did as she was instructed and, to her great relief, it worked. The noise had been so loud it was excruciatingly painful. She threw him a grateful look. "Thanks."

The source of the noise was immediately obvious, there next to an enormous waterfall thundering down the far side of this dark cavern, were white-hot furnaces lighting the cavern. The thudding resulted from the vast dark machinery heating the fearsome furnaces. Huge pistons thudded and cogs spun. Devlins were directing the black liquid into channels via a wooden trough, into each of the furnaces in turn. Frequently, the Devlins controlling the troughs were missing and spillages of the toxic black liquid fell onto unsuspecting Devlins below, with a harsh sizzling of repulsive leathery flesh. They were bellowing

Deep in her unconsciousness she heard Anuthel shouting her name, but missed him chuckling quietly "Well, I never, I do believe that's the Ferry of Goth Aref and if I'm not mistaken that's Rhianne herself at the helm. She's still up to her old tricks, then."

Emeriel roused slowly, sitting up as she fought dizziness and confusion, rearing to see what held Anuthel's attention. With indescribable relief, she realised that she could see Jes, Jenna and Jasper in a small boat in the waters far below.

"Jenna! Jes! Here!! Over here! Please!" She yelled as she waved frantically, but it was useless; they were so far away.

"They can't hear you because of the waves at the bottom of the cliffs and the smog. It's a wonder you can see them at all!"

"I don't care! Just tell me how can we get down there?" Emeriel pleaded, she was desperate to be reunited with them.

"Well. I don't know myself but I'm pretty sure Rhianne would?" He sighed.

"Rhianne? Oh, yes, Zithanduel's sister. She mentioned her." Emeriel was resigned to the fact she was not going to get their attention by shouting and getting agitated.

"She is also the Princess of Faerspring, though I'll bet your friends don't have a clue yet!" Anuthel smiled wistfully. "She is amazing, a mistress of disguise with a heart of Topazaio!"

"Well, why don't you summon her and ask her to help us. I know I can't." She said, somewhat impatiently.

Anuthel knew she was exhausted and urgently wanted to see her family. He glanced at the huge crater and the devastation below. It was gruesome. Some were headless but muddling around still mobile, their small brain not being an important nerve centre, and many lacked a limb or two.

They were no longer much of a threat but he still wondered whether their task was complete or not. They may have obviously foiled the plan to poison the springs but whether Lord Madded was dead or alive was of vital importance to the future of Faerspring.

Emeriel was oblivious to his thoughts, and though she acknowledged it was probably impossible, she was still trying to get the attention of the crew. "I don't see Jish."

Anuthel turned his attention toward the Ferry, puzzling for a few seconds and then proudly produced a rope from the depths of his pockets. She looked blankly at him and with exasperation. "OK, a rope but..."

"Not, any old rope, Emeriel. Watch!" He was excited, now. He walked with deliberation and high drama to the edge of the cliff and began to let the rope down. Despite its apparent shortness, it plummeted to the depths below.

Emeriel couldn't help commenting, "It would have been useful with the Boat Keeper!"

He glared and stated obviously, "We wouldn't have had it now though. Would we?"

Ignoring her, he whispered into the rope end he was holding, and much to Emeriel's astonishment, the rope wound its way around and into the Ferry, tapping Jes on the knee. He looked to see where the rope had come from. Emeriel watched as he realised she was on the cliff top and safe. The crew were jumping about wildly, almost overturning the Ferry.

"Emeriel, I have their attention." Nelida had fixed her far-seeing eyes fixed on Anuthel's and raised her hand in acknowledgment.

"Can you lift the boat with the rope, Anuthel?"

"No! I'm only a Dwarf!"

Emeriel looked at the craft. She knew she had no hidden Giffts to help, but perceived a stranger's thought, "That's right, Emeriel, but Jes has." And as Emeriel gazed on the scene at sea helplessly, she observed the old lady Anuthel had referred to as Rhianne, whisper into Jes' ear. She noticed in quiet amazement, holding her breath, as he focused on the boat, elevating it steadily, transporting it up the cliff.

Everyone was preoccupied, Jes focusing on the task, the remaining Crew and Emeriel being distracted with delight at seeing each other again. Nelida sensed Lord Madded spying on them from a distance on the cliff edge.

The Ferry landed safely, still a distance from Anuthel and Emeriel. Nelida said urgently, "I'm afraid we have company of the worst sort!"

Jes, Jenna and Jasper turned to see to whom she was referring. There was an ugly-looking, thick-skinned creature and they knew were looking at a Devlin. Jes felt an usually strong twinge in his arm at the proximity of such evil, the black pulse had quickened incredibly..

Emeriel and Anuthel, who had also just noticed him, gasped in synchrony, "Lord Madded!"

"He is their Leader and still here." Nelida stated. They all disembarked and rushed toward Emeriel.

Jenna arrived first and hugged her murmuring, "I thought I'd never see you again!" The advance of Lord Madded and several unharmed Devlins interrupted the joyful reunion.

"Any ideas?" Emeriel asked Anuthel, reverting once more to thought speech.

"Not right now!" He replied in terror, seeing the treacherous Leader again.

"But, I think I have," Nelida interjected, joining the private thought conversation.

Anuthel bowed low, "Princess Rhianne!"

She smiled at him and turned to greet Emeriel, "Pleased to meet you. I am Nelida to your friends; still no time for further introductions or explanations. Can we body cloak the others by linking hands around them? Then we can move off and plan how to be rid of the Devlins!"

Emeriel peered more closely, at the ancient looking Faerie and sensed she was not what she seemed, nevertheless her idea was a good one, and so gripping the bony fingers and Anuthel's podgy ones, in an instant, the group disappeared. They retreated from the cliff; invisible to the confused Devlins, though Lord Madded was sure he'd seen this trick before.

"He has to go! If he lives, he will continue with his wicked schemes and Faerspring will never be safe." Nelida communicated with Emeriel and Anuthel. They continued to edge back clumsily, making slow, steady progress. "Can you keep the body cloak with Anuthel, Emeriel? I will sort out Madded. I've been wanting to do this for some while."

Emeriel nodded, clasping Anuthel's other hand. Jes squeezed Jenna tightly. Jasper huddled closer. Jenna's foot made an intermittent appearance but Lord Madded was rather too occupied to notice. Emeriel watched Nelida making her way invisibly toward Lord Madded, her diminutive frame contrasting starkly with his bulk. She had almost reached him when, with a flash of intense, silvery light she transformed herself into Princess Rhianne, transflighting and towering above him. The light surrounding her was so bright he was clearly in awe of her and terrified.

Jes, Jenna and Jasper were also stunned to witness this transformation and also felt duped, though admittedly they were extremely relieved as well, of course. Lord Madded realised too late and was aghast, as he remembered her parents and their death, and knew how powerful she was.

"Madded," she spoke quietly, but it seemed to reverberate around the cliff top eerily. "Your time is over. You have been unpunished for too long. Justice has decreed you will die!" And though she was Faerspringian and of much good, she struck out with her hand and the silvery white light transformed into a fiery sword.

She thrust it into Lord Madded and his companions, in one swift movement. In that instant, they heard a loud, rushing noise like the sound of a thousand waterfalls, and a flaming bolt radiated from the sword and they were gone. At the same moment, the storm clouds vanished, the sea calmed and the sky lightened.

Wild celebration broke out immediately. Jes and Emeriel hugged. Jenna ran to join them. Rhianne came over to greet Anuthel.

Jes glanced at Rhianne saying, "You were secretive!"

"I've had to be! Now, we must ensure that no further damage is done." She said forcefully.

Emeriel nodded, "Yes! Anuthel and I saw Strychnopurine being poured into the deep underground waters, only a small amount but…."

Anuthel interrupted nodding, "It has infected the Great Spring. Until I saw it, I did not realise, I thought it was a myth, Princess, but Emeriel and I have seen, what must surely be, the Great Spring."

Rhianne agreed, "I suspected for some while, but had no evidence. My disguise helped me glean more information but sadly, not enough to prevent this, it would seem. However, we have a chance, if we act quickly!"

She took out the crystal orb and summoned Jeruthel. "Send Loro at once. Ensure no-one drinks any of the waters in Nilhspring until I have sent a Priest from the Temple of Ecurelian to purify them. They have been poisoned."

Then in turn she contacted the Spring Keepers in Welhspring, Elhspring and Silhspring. In the time it took her to do this, though she was brief and efficient, Loro could be seen in the distance.

Rhianne rapped out her instructions. "We do not have time on our side. Loro must fetch the Priests of Ecurelian. Even so, how are we going to ensure they reach each of the Springs in time? The Citizens will die of thirst!"

"Could you communicate with the Priests and ask them if there is another way?" Emeriel offered tentatively. She had not met Rhianne before and was less intimidated than the others.

"Yes! Excellent" Rhianne was impressed.

She gazed into the orb once more. "Great Priest of Ecurelian, Princess Rhianne of Faerspring, seeks your help!" She tapped the orb gently and a surprisingly young pale faced being appeared.

He had the palest grey eyes and appeared translucent, the marble walled room clearly visible behind him. He had straight blonde hair; so long it was not possible to see where it finished; they could only see his profile. With a serious expression, he responded, though his lips did not move, "You called Princess? It must be urgent. We have not spoken in many Faercenturies. How may we of Ecurelian serve you?" He nodded courteously. Emeriel could see the others had heard, so he could not be using thought speech.

"Greetings!" Rhianne returned his nod respectfully and submissively. Jes couldn't help thinking she looked almost servant-like as she explained the situation to the Great Priest.

He did not look surprised and simply replied, "We were ready. Our archives foretold of this and we have been following the journey from our copy of the Ancient Book of Lore. We were expecting your request. You need the Gems of Purification. We have them here and on the command of the Chosen One, we can transwill them to you."

Emeriel and Jenna gasped jointly on hearing this. They both knew they were not able to do this. Rhianne looked piercingly at Jes and said, "We need your help." Jes nodded. He knew he had this Gifft but could he utilise it under such pressure?

He stepped forward, took the orb from Rhianne and knelt down bowing his head. He whispered softly, "Gems of Purification, in the Name of Justice, come forth," as he steadily stretched out his hand toward the orb an intense bolt of purple lightening shot from it and five perfect egg-shaped gems of deepest blue appeared in his hand. He cupped both hands deftly around them, leaving the orb suspended in the air.

The Priest continued, as though it was an every pel event, "There is a Gem for each Spring including the Great Spring. You will need the Lorduress and another two of his companions.

"Rhianne, you must go to Nilhspring yourself and each of the Chosen Ones to a Spring. The Gems should be thrown into each Spring Source. You will know they have been purified because the waters will turn blue and then become clear again. Any citizen drinking from the Springs before this has happened will perish.

" We will make petitions to Justice whilst you accomplish your task. I will go and summon the Frerehood. Our time has come!" and with that, he vanished.

Princess Rhianne turned to speak but Loro was fast approaching, and as they were used to his landings, the entire group scattered and ran for cover to his great amusement. He was delighted to see them.

"Loro!" Rhianne quickly regained control, "We need you and two of your fellows!" Loro nodded he was ever the obedient servant of the Princess; he remembered her parents well and had vowed after their deaths to take care of her. He knew from the Dragon Lore, she would need him and his kind. He immediately departed at speed.

But as they watched, they were stunned to see him fly vertically upwards, in a way he had never done before, and then in a puff of hazy, black smoke he disappeared from view, returning moments later with two mighty companions, one slightly smaller than he and one much chubbier.

Alarmingly, they headed vertically downwards and the group scattered for a second time. The trio landed inelegantly, in a tangled pile, but were soon on their feet, albeit with puffing and panting smoke and fire from their nostrils after their exertions.

"We meet again, Rolo!" Rhianne patted the smaller Lorduress affectionately on his nuzzle. He returned her smile, fangs exposed in a friendly grin. To the other, she said, "Nolly! I have missed you." The chubby lorduress winked at her mischievously. "Friends, we must hurry. Emeriel, you must go with Nolly to Silhspring, Jenna…Loro… Elhspring. Jes… Rolo…. Welhspring. Ask for the Spring Keeper, they will be expecting you. I will go to Nilhspring and we will meet later in Welhspring. Jasper and Anuthel I want you to round up any remaining Devlins and purify the Great Spring. I will send help from Nilhspring."

"What about the Devlins outside Faerspring?" Emeriel asked.

Again, Rhianne was impressed. "Yes. I've been thinking about that too. Difficult. There must be a…"

Anuthel chuckled as he produced a lump of black coal-like rock.

"What is that?" Emeriel wanted to know, though she suspected already.

"Solid Strychnopurine." He replied rather pleased with himself.

Rhianne took charge, "After you have dealt with the situation here, take it to the Master Gifft Scholars they will know what to do with it."

By midpel, the tasks in each of the Springs were completed and the remaining Devlins had been despatched to the Nether World with the help of the Master Gifft Scholars..

Chapter Twenty-Two

The Homecoming

Jes and Rolo found a Welcoming Party, which included Zithanduel and an elderly-looking Spring Keeper, on the glass platform. Expecting them, Zithanduel instructed the Spring Keeper to lead Jes to the Spring's source, deep within the crystal structure. Again, he felt mesmerised by the beauty of the blue water reflected through the crystal layers. It was hard to conceive that these waters could be poisoned.

The Spring Keeper brought him to the rock face that Methven had previously taken them to and tapped the wall further along. A door opened silently revealing a spring gushing into a marble pool arising from unseen depths. A stream flowed into the rocks beyond, feeding the channels, which flowed throughout Welhspring. Quite how gravity came into it, Jes was unsure but like many sights on Faerspring, he accepted it at face value. There was the faintest of twinges at his arm as he neared the spring and surreptitiously checking the Mark it confirmed the Spring was affected.

He took the crystal carefully from his pouch and threw it into the pool. It turned deep purple with a loud hiss and an engulfing thick vapour filled the cavern and then vanished. The waters ran clear again. The Mark of Justice had regained its faint blue hue and he felt tremendous pressure lift.

"It is done!" The Spring Keeper sounded relieved and Jes knew he had been in contact with Rhianne. "We are proud of your achievements. You must be very tired. Zithanduel has asked me to take you to your quarters and you can rest. I'll send Gerianne along shortly. The others will be a while yet I expect."

Jes transflighted behind him and could not help feeling an empty sadness at Methven's loss, as they travelled along now familiar corridors, when he considered all that had happened in the last few pel. He felt wonderment, too, at what he had learned and achieved. They had just reached the door, when Emeriel and Zithanduel appeared.

"How come you were so quick?" he asked Emeriel intrigued at her speedy return.

"Nolly was quite something in the air, though he looked clumsy and slow."

Zithanduel smiled at this, "Nolly used to win the Lorduress Yerual Event in the Faerspring Olymia Festival, every yer when my parents were alive." Gerianne arrived and opened the rock door. Zithanduel left them politely, followed by the Spring Keeper; she could see Emeriel and Jes had much to catch up on. Emeriel and Jes smiled at each other as they went in.

Gerianne looked at them both with appreciation, "We are indebted to you. I am so glad you are safe."

The spotless room was welcoming and familiar. Without delay, Emeriel raced over to the hammock pedestal and was relaxing, thoughtfully, on the gold hammock, in moments. Jes followed suite. Gerianne prepared some Emerene and brought it over to each of them.

"I believe Jenna has just arrived. I will fetch her."

He vanished then and returned shortly with Jenna. She hugged Emeriel and Jes enthusiastically, followed energetically by Torro and Renewil though how she managed to bring them from Elhspring was not clear and nobody cared. They were so relieved to be together. Gerianne prepared the table for a meal and opened the drapes so that they could enjoy the view of the setting suns,

"I'll leave you to enjoy your meal in peace."

"Where's Methven?" Emeriel asked. Jenna's eyes filled with tears. Jes and Jenna took it in turns to tell Emeriel events since her abduction. Emeriel recounted her own adventures on Goth Malin. Jes tried to explain to them both about the Mark of Justice but his own understanding was still limited. He had to share the burden with them though. The suns set. Gerianne returned, cleared the meal away and prepared the room for nel.

"You must rest now. It will be a special pel on the morrow. A Festival of Victory and Celebration will be held in your honour. Zithanduel insists I ensure you sleep."

They did not argue. They uttered not one more word. They undressed, putting on the finest nelwear ever and cosied into the softest hammock ever, falling asleep immediately. They dreamed of Goth Malin, the Springs, the Ilves and Dwarves and of, long forgotten, home.

Strangely, when they awoke the next pel, they each expected to wake at home but Gerianne appeared and made them a magnificent pelfirst. He operated a pedestal revealing ceremonial gowns, tunics and newly made, soft, hide shoes. He led them to a pool adjacent to their room, where they bathed and dressed. It was bliss after their travels even Jes enjoyed it.

Finally, Gerianne announced formally, " The Citizens of Faerspring await!"

They transflighted behind him, so adept in the skill now that even an outsider would assume they were native. They passed the Glade of Gillelien and approached the Great Hall. This time it was filled to capacity, with not only Faeries, but also Ilves, Dwarves and Loro too.

As soon as they made their entrance, the conversational buzz was silenced by a spreading hush of awe and respect. All greeted them with a Faerspring Bow, even Loro, which had Jenna in secret kinks and they felt extremely honoured, especially with the thunderous applause that followed, continuing ad infinitum. They felt humbled and appreciated.

Zithanduel elevated herself above the assembly.

"Honoured friends, Citizens of Welhspring and Guests from Faerspring and beyond, we welcome you to this special gathering to celebrate our victory over the Devlins. The Springs are pure once more and the threat to them has been removed by the Chosen Ones. We retain our immortality. We owe them our gratitude and are indebted to them.

"We are also grateful to the Lorduress, as ever for their service and courage. We must also express our thanks to Anuthel the Ancient, for his courage and for remaining loyal and steadfast to the cause, especially during his long years of imprisonment.

"I am glad to welcome Rhianne to Welhspring after some time away and am aware that she wishes to address you all." She transflighted to the

Emeriel! "…It is fitting that they should have tokens of our appreciation by which to remember us…"

Three members of the Council of the Gathring, Emanuain, Omendar and Glerendel, in their ceremonial robes appeared with beautifully crafted presentation cushions, of Ilvish design and upon which were laid wristbands woven in gold and silver and studded with Topazio jewels from the Nilhspring Mynes. Rhianne placed them on their wrists, one by one. The moment they were on they reverted to Ellie, Thomas and Joanne. The audience erupted cheering, applauding and giving Faerspring Bows.

"My friends, we would like you to remain here with us and continue to defend us."

Ellie, Tom and Jo suddenly felt bewildered and quite shy, especially Ellie who had never liked being out in front of so many people.

Tom looked at Ellie who nodded as he started to speak, "We are very grateful for the wristbands and your kind offer but we have family and friends on our world, far away from this beautiful place. We will miss you all and your generosity, but if you are able to grant it, we would like to go home. The bracelets are truly wonderful and they have enabled us to see, clearly, where we belong."

Rhianne smiled knowingly, "We give you leave to return whenever you chose, for our help. Justice has already permitted me to grant you this and to allow your wish to leave. Please follow me." The cheering and roaring continued long after they left with Rhianne, as did the eating, dancing and celebrating!

Rhianne led them onto a magnificent balcony, overlooking the valley below and the glass platform was nearby. Jasper, Jish, Loro, Torro, Renewil, Anuthel, Jeruthel and Ruthven had all followed and now stood with them. Zithanduel and Ariella transfigured alongside Rhianne.

"We knew you would need to leave. It was written in a Chapter of the Lore, which became plain to me last night. We are saddened, but realise you must return to your home. Justice has given Jish back to us and we are grateful for that.

"We still mourn Methven's passing and Justice has not seen fit to grant our petition for his return. We must be patient. We know we may not have destroyed all the Devlins. They may try to regroup but we shall be ever vigilant and keep Goth Malin under close inspection."

Rhianne glanced over at Jeruthel and Loro who confirmed their willingness to do this. "We know, also, that we have other enemies but we continue in peace for now and we thank you for that. If you stand on the platform, you will be at the tunnel entrance in a few moments."

Ellie, Tom and Jo hugged each of their friends in turn.

They looked out across Faerspring, the valleys and mountains and were struck by the beauty once more; the water, streams and zellifers below. The moons of Faerspring were now rising and a green silent glow fell across the land they had come to love. They walked through the balcony gate, onto the platform. Renewil fluttered nearby. Loro had enormous tears rolling down his cheeks and Torro had matching smaller ones. The platform moved away from the balcony.

Shockingly, they witnessed a sight that stunned them. Rhianne, Zithanduel and Ariella merged into one figure, as they waved farewell. Ellie felt compelled to touch her bracelet for a moment and as she did so she knew that she was being allowed to share Rhianne's thoughts on this occasion.

"We are one and the same, only a few know."

"Anuthel?"

"And Jeruthel and Loro."

"I don't understand. Why?"

"When my parents died, sadly my sisters went with them. Only Loro witnessed it. Even in the depths of my grief, I knew Faerspring would be devastated and ruling Faerspring would be difficult. Justice suggested it, as a way of avoiding the chaos…

Despite the increasing distance between them, Emeriel caught a final, "Farewell…until we meet again."

"Goodbye," Emeriel returned the thought.

The others were puzzled at what they had seen, and Ellie tried to explain what she had learned as the platform increased its speed and entered a thick, dense cloud. A green velvety darkness enfolded them and they spiralled into blackness.

Ellie opened her eyes and could hear a bell in the distance. It was Grandma's bell she realised with enormous relief, looking up at the fern-covered dell and then across at a dazed Tom and puzzled Jo.

They gazed back at her. She touched the friendship bracelet of silver and gold thread at her wrist and 'heard' Tom think, "I didn't have a bracelet, like this before…. Nor a freckle that colour!" He looked at his arm in confusion.

"No, you didn't Tom." She replied silently.

**Difficult Words Explained** – _to save you looking them up!_

abject	downcast, humiliated
accentuated	emphasised, draws attention to
accomplish	achieve, complete successfully
acknowledge	recognise that something is right or true
acquaintance	someone one knows but not closely
acquiesce	agree without being said
acute	sharp, serious
ad infinitum	forever, without limit
adamant	insistent, firm
administration	management of business affairs
adversaries	enemies
agility	nimbleness, speed
ailments	illnesses
alabaster	type of gypsum that is white and opaque or translucent
amiable	likeable, friendly
anticipate	expect
aperture	opening
apparition	appearance of a supernatural being; ghost
apprehensive	worried, uneasy, anxious
astute	cunning, clever
austere	stern, severely simple
azure	blue
bail	remove water from bottom of boat
bemused	lost in thought, dazed, confused
bilious	derangement of the bile, bile is a bitter yellow body fluid
bluffed	pretended, lied
botanical	plant-like
brazier	stand or pan for holding hot coals
brooding	thinking or worrying about for a long time
brusquely	curt, brisk, abrupt
bulbous	rounded like a bulb
burly	sturdy, big, strong
cascaded	falling in folds or drapes
circumspectly	warily, cautiously, taking everything into account
citadel	stronghold, refuge, castle
clad	covered, clothed
cognizant	aware of
commotion	disturbance, uproar
composure	calmness of mind, serenity

concealed	hidden, secret
conscientious	hard working, paying attention to conscience
consequences	effect or result
consolation	comfort in distress or grief
conspicuous	easily seen, noticeable
constellation	star group
contemplations	mental viewing, thoughtful considerations
contradictory	opposite
contretemps	unexpected mishap, unlucky occurrence
coursing	moving, running
crenellated	indented spaces on a battlement or parapet
crevasse	deep cleft in ice or snow
curtness	shortness, rudely brief
cynical	sceptical, distrusting
dais	raised platform in hall for a high table or throne
deciphering	decode, make out the meaning of
decoy	something used to attract or lure others into a trap
decreed	officially commanded
deduced	drew as a conclusion from the facts
degenerate	deteriorate
demise	death
density	thickness
desolation	abandonment, loneliness
despondent	lacking hope or courage, sad
dialect	regional variation of a language
diligence	persistent effort or work
dimension	particular aspect
diminutive	tiny, small
discern	distinguish, see clearly
disconcerting	taking aback or dismaying
disembarked	go ashore, get off
dishevelled	untidy, scruffy
dismissive	send away, giving only brief consideration to
disorientating	confusing to bearings or sense of what is right
dispersed	scattered, spread widely
dumbfounded	amazed into silence
earnest	sincere, determined
ecstasy	extreme excitement
effluvium	exhaled unpleasant substance affecting lungs or sense of smell
elusive	hard to find or catch
emanating	coming from
encompassing	surrounding, forming circle around

encounter	*meeting*
engulf	*swallow up*
enshrouded	*covered*
ensued	*come about or follow especially as consequence*
entreat	*implore, beg*
eradicate	*wipe out*
espied	*caught sight of*
ethereal	*heavenly, light and airy*
excrement	*waste matter discharged from the body*
expire	*die*
fledgling	*inexperienced person, young*
fleetingly	*briefly, transiently*
flourishing	*thrive, grow healthily*
foreboding	*dread, sense of coming evil*
forlorn	*deserted, miserable*
formidable	*fearful, threatening*
futile	*pointless*
garland	*flowers woven into a ring for the head or neck*
gossamer	*light, filmy, delicate substance*
grotesque	*extremely ugly*
guffaw	*coarse or boisterous laugh*
guttural	*coming from the throat*
hailed	*to be native of*
hallowed	*holy, respected*
harboured	*held secret, cherish*
hitherto	*previously*
holograms	*two or three dimensional light pattern*
homage	*act of respect or reverence given to someone*
hysterically	*panicking uncontrollably*
imparted	*made information or news known*
impenetrable	*that cannot be penetrated or passed through*
imperative	*urgent, essential, commanding*
impotently	*powerlessly, helplessly*
inaudible	*that which cannot be heard*
incandescent	*glowing with heat; shining brightly*
incensed	*enraged, furious*
incongruous	*out of place, not suitable*
inexplicably	*without explanation*
innate	*existing in person from birth, natural, inherent*
insignificant	*unimportant*
intimidated	*discouraged by threats, frightened*
intuition	*ability to understand and perceive things instinctively*
invocation	*calling upon a higher being*

iridescent	*shimmering with rainbow colours*
languorously	*exhaustedly, droopingly, faintly*
leaden	*heavy, sluggish*
legible	*readable*
lush	*densely growing*
mammoth	*huge, enormous*
manoeuvred	*move or cause to move in desired direction*
meandered	*wander, follow a winding course*
mesmerising	*hypnotizing, fascinating greatly*
millennia	*thousands of yers*
minimised	*reduced*
minion	*employee or follower especially subordinate*
misgivings	*concerns, worries*
monologue	*long speech by one person*
multifaceted	*many aspects*
multitudinous	*many*
myriad	*great number*
navigating	*following the course*
nebulous	*cloud-like, hazy, vague*
negotiating	*reaching an agreement through discussion*
noxious	*poisonous*
oblivion	*forgotten state, disregarded*
oblivious	*unaware*
obscured	*hidden*
ode	*poem addressed to particular person or object*
odorous	*smelly*
opalescent	*showing changing colours like opal*
oppressive	*harsh, cruel, weighing down*
optimistic	*hopeful, expecting the best will happen*
overbearing	*bossy, domineering*
painstakingly	*carefully, meticulously*
panoramic	*unbroken view of wide area*
paralysed	*unable to move*
perceptible	*noticeable, discernible*
perfunctory	*done as though getting through a duty*
perilously	*dangerously, life threateningly*
perimeter	*boundary, circumference*
perish	*die*
permeate	*spread through, pervading*
permitted	*allowed*
perpendicular	*at right angles to the horizon*
perspective	*view, prospect*
pervert	*turn from proper use, corrupt*

petition	*make or receive a humble or formal request*
phosphorescence	*emitting or giving out a faint light*
pilgrims	*those who journey to a sacred place*
pivotal	*dependant on or turning upon, critical*
precarious	*unsafe, uncertain, insecure*
predicament	*awkward or dangerous situation*
promontory	*headland*
prow	*the projecting front of boat*
proximity	*nearness*
prudently	*wisely, cautious*
pursued	*follow with intent*
queasy	*feeling nausea, sickly*
quest	*a fervent search or hunt, one's goal*
rampant	*rife, unchecked*
rancid	*having an unpleasant stale smell or taste*
rapport	*good communication, harmonious relationship*
rapturous	*ecstatic delight, pleasure*
ravine	*steep, narrow valley, mountain cleft*
reeling	*staggering, swaying*
refectory	*large communal dining hall*
regaling	*entertaining choicely often with food or talk*
rendition	*version or interpretation of*
renowned	*well-known*
reprimand	*severe scold or telling-off*
reprisal	*retaliation*
reproach	*scold, rebuke, tell-off*
repulsive	*disgusting, distasteful*
resolute	*determined, firm*
reverberated	*vibrate noisily, echo*
reverie	*abstract musing, thoughts*
reverted	*return to former state or condition*
ritualistic	*ceremonial, procedure*
rotundly	*roundly*
ruefully	*regretfully*
sacrificed	*gave up something so that greater good may result*
scrutinising	*examining closely, carefully, in detail*
simultaneously	*at the same time*
speculating	*theorizing, reflectively*
sporadic	*occasional, occurring irregularly*
stalactites	*deposit of calcium carbonate rock hanging like icicle from roof of cave*
stalagmites	*as above but standing on floor of cave*
stance	*position, pose*

stench	foul smell
subdued	put down, quietened
submissively	timidly, giving up
subterranean	underground
summoned	commanded to be present
surly	bad-tempered, unhelpful
surreptitiously	done in a way deliberately concealing or hiding
synchrony	working or occurring at the same time
tenaciously	holding or sticking firmly
tirade	long, angry speech
tortuous	winding, twisting
transiently	briefly
translucent	transmitting light but not see-through
traversing	crossing from one side or corner to another
treacherous	dangerous, hazardous
turmoil	state of confusion
uncharitable	severe in judgement, unkind in understanding
unhindered	not stopped, no barrier
utilise	make practical or worthwhile use of
vacant	empty
vacuum	a space without air
valiant	brave
vantage	advantageous position for defence or attack
verdant	fresh coloured, green, covered with grass
vermilion	red
vigilant	watchful, alert
vista	long narrow view into the distance
vitality	energy, strength
voracious	greedy in eating, ravenous
vortex	whirling motion or mass
waning	decreasing
wielding	holding and using, possessing
wizened	shrivelled, dried up appearance

Words from the Faerspring Lore

balsaid	_lightweight wood used for making boats which comes from Limebrack trees_
clospel	_colour from the Faerspring spectrum of light_
Elh	_equivalent to East on earth_
Faercentury	_a hundred yers_
Faergallon	_unit of measure for liquids equivalent to few earth litres_
Faermatres	_unit of measure_
Faermills	_unit of distance_
flers	_another unit of time ten flers make a yer_
Gathring	_the council of Faerspring composed of trusted allies of the High Chieftanna_
Giffts	_special abilities given to certain individuals by Justice; to be used wisely for the good of Faerspring_
halfpel	_half a pel_
iridichium	_colour from the Faerspring spectrum of light_
midpel	_midday_
nel	_night_
nelfall	_nightfall_
nelsky	_night sky_
nelwear	_nightwear_
Nilh	_equivalent to North on earth_
pel	_Faerspring unit of time equivalent to day, twenty five pel make one fler_
peleve	_evening_
pelfirst	_breakfast_
pellun	_lunch_
quartpel	_short amount of Faerspring time, a quarter of a pel_
rosper	_colour from the Faerspring spectrum of light_
Silh	_equivalent to South on earth_
Topazaio	_precious gem of Faerspring_
topel	_today_
transfigure	_Gifft of transferring oneself from one place to another instantly and invisibly_
tyranghelli	_winged copper coloured creatures_
Welh	_equivalent to West on earth_
yers	_a Faerspring measure of time_
yesterpel	_yesterday_
zellifer	_horse-like creatures with green/yellow stripes_

There are many other new and strange words within the Lore but these will be enough to speed you on your way into Faerspring.

Jasper's Explanation of the Ancient Lore Symbols for Emeriel

a b c d e f g h i j k l m n o p q r s t u v w x y z

α β χ δ ε φ γ η ι φ κ λ μ ν ο π θ ρ σ τ υ ϖ ω ξ ψ ζ

A B C D E F G H I J K L M N O P Q R S T U V W X Y Z

Α Β Χ Δ Ε Φ Γ Η Ι ϑ Κ Λ Μ Ν Ο Π Θ Ρ Σ Τ Υ ς Ω Ξ Ψ Ζ

I hope you enjoyed Angel of Justice

Look out for

Book 2 from the Lore of Faerspring

"ANUTHEL OF JEZZITHRA!"

due to be published in June 2004.

For details check out www.angelofjustice.com